MW01181334

A Visitor to Heaven's Garden of Blessings

JOYCE M. ENGLEHARDT

WestBow
PRESS
A DIVISION OF THOMAS NELSON

Copyright © 2011 by Joyce M. Englehardt.

All rights reserved. No part of this book may be used or reproduced by any means, graphic, electronic, or mechanical, including photocopying, recording, taping or by any information storage retrieval system without the written permission of the publisher except in the case of brief quotations embodied in critical articles and reviews.

The information, ideas, and suggestions in this book are not intended as a substitute for professional medical advice. Before following any suggestions contained in this book, you should consult your personal physician. Neither the author nor the publisher shall be liable or responsible for any loss or damage allegedly arising as a consequence of your use or application of any information or suggestions in this book.

WestBow Press books may be ordered through booksellers or by contacting:

WestBow Press
A Division of Thomas Nelson
1663 Liberty Drive
Bloomington, IN 47403
www.westbowpress.com
1-(866) 928-1240

Because of the dynamic nature of the Internet, any web addresses or links contained in this book may have changed since publication and may no longer be valid. The views expressed in this work are solely those of the author and do not necessarily reflect the views of the publisher, and the publisher hereby disclaims any responsibility for them.

Any people depicted in stock imagery provided by Thinkstock are models, and such images are being used for illustrative purposes only.

Certain stock imagery © Thinkstock.

ISBN: 978-1-4497-2583-9 (sc)
ISBN: 978-1-4497-2584-6 (hc)
ISBN: 978-1-4497-2582-2 (ebk)
Library of Congress Control Number: 2011915387

Printed in the United States of America

WestBow Press rev. date: 08/30/2011

To my own special daughter

Tawny Marie Kidd

And to

That Special Bond, between

Mothers and Daughters everywhere:

Also to my son

Daniel Joel Applegate

And granddaughter

Rachel Anna Miller

And a big thank you to Barbara Ray,

For her much needed help.

Dear reader, I would like to take a moment to say, that this is a book of fiction. It was however inspired. It started with a dream that was so vivid that I decided to write down the basic concept of the dream. The next thing I knew I was writing a book.

This is a story about two couples that meet and support each other, through some very hard times.

I didn't give a town or a city for my characters because where they lived was not important. What they went through could have happened anywhere in America.

I don't pretend to understand comas. I only know that there have been miracles. And this book is about miracles, and hanging on to the promises of God. I hope it will bless you.

Forward and Testimony

Many people who consider themselves Christians proclaim that miracles have passed away. It is difficult for them to believe for a miracle if they have been taught it is the will of God for them to suffer sickness and disease. There are however, many of us who have experienced the supernatural power of God in our own lives and we know that miracles are available to all of us and not just for "special people".

When our four year old daughter was in a coma with a bullet wound to the head, we knew we were a candidate for God's supernatural intervention. While she lay in intensive care unconscious, we read the healing scriptures to her knowing it was God's will for her to be healed and believing that God would watch over His Word to perform it. Jeremiah 30:17 was the Bible verse we proclaimed, "I will restore health unto you and heal you of your wounds." Thirty hours later she opened her eyes, healed by the supernatural power of God!

My prayer is that the book, "A Visitor to Heaven's Garden of Blessings", by Joyce Englehardt, will encourage and strengthen your faith to believe in a God who can change the natural course of events by His unexplainable power and bring about a miracle in your life. Peggy Hedgpeth

Matt 4:23 *(And Jesus was going about in all Galilee, teaching in their synagogues, and proclaiming the gospel of the kingdom, and healing every kind of disease and every kind of sickness among the people.)*

Introduction

◆

This story first came to me in the form of a dream. In my dream, I see two little girls in the hospital. They are both in comas. I watch as their mothers deal with what is happening.

The first little girl Amy was brought in when she was just five and has been in a coma for nearly two years, and yet her mother, Lil Iverson seems to have total peace that Amy will come back to her. Amy is a quick—witted child with a wonderful sense of humor. She has always been full of life and very active, she loves to run and climb. Some would say she's a tomboy. Amy has beautiful bronze curls just like her mom. Lil has had many dreams in which she is able to visit with Amy in a heavenly garden and actually watch her grow.

The other little girl Melisa has only been in the hospital a couple of days. And her mother, Debbie Miller is having a very hard time accepting what has happened to her little girl: she is angry with God because just a couple of days ago Missy was at home playing with her friends. How could God allow this to happen? Missy is a more quiet and reflective child. She is very sensitive and loves her dolls and story books. Melisa is a beautiful little girl with dark brown hair like her papa and she's also very smart.

Lil is a lovely, strong Christian woman who is filled with faith. And she talks to her daughter as if she can hear every word. She also talks to God as if He can hear every word.

Debbie admires Lil's faith, but she still doesn't understand how this mother can be so upbeat when her daughter is lying there in a coma.

Lil is being very patient with Debbie, because she knows how hard it is to accept tragedy when it comes into our lives. She also knows that the Lord has the answers to all of Debbie's questions. So she continues to quietly witness to Debra and to pray that the Lord will open her heart to God's truth. "Please Lord give me wisdom as I reach out to Debra. Help me to say the right things, the things you want her to hear. I ask this in Jesus name. Amen"

Part One
The Iversons and the Millers

Chapter One

———————————◆———————————

The book I'm reading is a children's book about a special garden, and I am sitting in a lovely garden surrounded by the most beautiful flowers I have ever seen.

I read, *("Toby look, there is a praying mantis. Be careful, I don't want you to hurt it. Oh Toby, isn't this fun? I love playing in the garden with you") . . . .*

I hear someone calling me. I look up from my reading to see Amy.

"Mommy, what are you doing?"

"Hi darling, I'm reading a lovely story about a little girl that likes to run with her kitten through the flowers and she finds all kinds of interesting things in the garden. How are you doing sweetheart?"

"I'm doing fine Mommy, but there's a new little girl here, and she's sad and a little bit scared. So I will be spending a lot of time with her."

"Oh, that is so thoughtful of you Amy . . . . Amy I . . . ."

Suddenly, Lil starts awake, still saying her daughter's name. "Amy, oh Amy, I so wish you could stay with me when I wake up. Dear Lord, I do appreciate the time I get to spend with Amy in the dreams, but I still wish for more."

Lil gets out of bed, and gets herself dressed and ready for her day. She has much to do. She has her coffee and toast and then heads for the door with her keys. Lil stops and picks up the little plush kitten she bought for Amy. "Amy will love this little kitty."

In the car Lil thinks back to that day almost two years ago when everything was as it should be. Their daughter was running and playing, and her laughter filled the air. It was hard not to ask why, and not to question how this could happen. Lil pulls into the hospital parking lot. She sits there for a moment to gather her thoughts and to ask God for the strength she will need for another day.

Once inside, she smiles down at Amy and says, "Hello darling. How is my sweet girl? I brought you the stuffed kitten I told you about. You will have to give him a name. He is all white except for a little black spot on his forehead."

Gladys, the warm hearted nurse that is more like a grandmother to Amy than she is her nurse, came into the room and greeted Lil with a smile. Lil asks her, "How did Amy do last night?"

Gladys shook her soft brown curls and said, "She is absolutely amazin'. At times, I'm sure she hears everythin' I say to her."

"Oh Gladys," Lil says, "I'm sure that she does, and she will be coming back to us very soon."

All of a sudden there is a commotion out in the hall. They both rush out to see what is happening. There is a lady standing there, who is very upset. She's saying, "But I saw her move, doctor. I am sure she moved." The doctor is saying something about muscle reflexes and trying to explain that this sometimes happens with patients that are in comas.

As Lil watches the mother, she understands exactly what she is going through. She also knows that doctors and medicine can only do so much. She looks into the room and sees a pretty little dark haired girl lying in the bed. She thinks this must be the little girl that Amy mentioned . . . .

After the doctor leaves, Debbie walks back into her daughter's room. And as she looks at her little girl and she can't help but wonder why. Why has this happened to us?

She remembers, it was just a couple of days ago that Melisa had been at home lying in her own bed with a slight fever . . . .

Missy had asked, "Mama, can I come out and watch TV with you? I'm feeling much better since you gave me that medicine."

Debra said, "No honey, not yet. It's much too soon. You have been a sick little girl and we have to get that fever down."

"Please Mama . . . . Papa, tell her I'm better. Feel my head. It's not near as hot as it was."

David turned to look at Debbie, and they exchange an unspoken worried look. Then he said, "You just need a little more time Missy and you will be as good as new."

"Do you promise, Papa?"

David answered, "I do promise. Now I want you get some sleep."

Missy pouted just a little before she said, "Okay, Papa. Good night Mama, I love you."

"We love you too Missy." they both chimed in together. They were a little worried, but not that much. Kids get fevers all the time.

After Debra finished up with the dishes she went back to check on Missy. "Oh, dear God," she cried out. And then she called to David who came running. "She's much worse David; call the doctor to meet us at the hospital." And so they rushed Missy to the hospital where they worked to get the fever down, but she lapsed into a coma.

The doctors could make no promises. They would continue to treat the virus and monitor her. Then they suggested that perhaps David and Debra should pray.

"Oh Debbie, I'm so sorry. I promised her she would be good as new."

"I know, David. It's not your fault. It's not anyone's fault. The first thing I did was to call out to God, but I don't even know if I believe that there is a God. We can't lose her David, we just can't."

It was the next day when Debbie saw Melisa move. The doctor said that nothing had changed on the monitors . . . .

Lil waited a while until things settled down. Then she approached Debra and said, "My little girl is right next door to yours if you need someone to talk to. I'm right here most every day. I know it is very hard, but if you need someone who understands, I'll be more than happy to listen."

Debbie looked up with a blank stare, but she didn't speak. She just shook her head and went back to watching her daughter.

Lil understood. She had long ago taken those first difficult steps back from her own tragedy and she understood it was very hard.

Just two years earlier things in the Iverson's home had been nearly perfect. Peter and Lil had a good marriage. They both had good jobs. Lil had her own dress shop, designing and making many of the clothes she sold. Peter was doing well with one of the top realtors in town. They owned a nice home on a couple of acres with just enough room for Amy's pony. They still had all that. They just needed Amy back.

Lil's thoughts drifted back, as she remembered how Amy had always been a tomboy; she loved playing ball and climbing trees. They had this one big old oak tree in the front yard and she just wouldn't leave her daddy alone until he built her a tree house.

Lil had worried about the pony and the tree house but Amy never had one bit of trouble climbing or riding, and they were always there to supervise.

They couldn't believe it when she slipped on the wet pavement and hit her head on her way to the park. The doctors said it was a mild concussion, she should be okay. They said everything looked good. She just didn't wake up.

Days turned into weeks and then months went by. Lil turned her shop over to a manager so she could work daily with the therapist to keep Amy's muscles working . . . .

It broke their hearts to see the pony with no one to ride it. So they gave it to a neighbor that has two little boys with the stipulation that as soon as Amy was awake she would have first dibs to ride. And except for a few pieces of play furniture, the tree house sat empty. It was all so sad, but all they could do was go on.

On the same day that Lil had tried to talk with Debra, she took a nap on one of the couches . . . .

Soon I was back in the garden with the butterflies and birds singing.

"I love the kitty Mommy; I'm going to name him Toby. He looks like a Toby don't you think?" . . . .

"Yes I guess he does, but how did you know that name?" I asked.

"Oh Mommy don't be silly, it's in the book you always read. You know the one about the special garden."

"Yes, of course it is, I just wasn't aware that you knew about it. Amy darling, remember when you told me about a new little girl that was here with you?"

"Yes Mommy, I know. Her name is Melisa and she's younger than me."

I responded, "Yes, that's the one and I'm so glad that she has you to help her. I hope she isn't frightened any more . . . . I hope she isn't . . . ."

"Wake up Lil, you were dreaming."

"Oh Peter, yes I was dreaming about Amy again. And Peter, she knew about the stuffed kitten I took her this morning. And the strangest thing happened. She named the kitty out of the book that I read when I'm there in the garden, and . . . ."

"Well, that makes sense to me. That is where you spend time with her, is in your dreams, right."

"Yes, but Peter I don't think I've ever read to her out of the book when I'm there."

"I'm sure I don't know dear, but I think you should just feel lucky that you are able to see her in that way. I sure wish I could!"

"No Peter, it's not luck. It's a blessing from God. Maybe you should pray and ask God that you might be able to see Amy in your dreams."

Peter answered, "Maybe I will. Now let's go see how our girl is doing."

Later as Lil sat by Amy she was thinking, I know I have told several people about my dreams and how it seems to me that Amy is actually growing taller and even looks a little older in these dreams. Lord, I can't help feeling that there's got to be more to it than just dreaming. It seems so real and then there's the way she knows things; things that are happening here in the hospital. She knew about Melisa and she even knew her name.

Then Lil prayed, "Dear God, I really want to help Debra deal with her situation, and to show her she needs to put her trust in you."

Lil continued to reach out to Debbie and she did open up a little, but whenever Lil would try to bring the Lord into their conversations Debra would always cut her off.

One evening after Lil had gone on home for the night, Debbie was talking to Gladys and she said to her, "I just don't understand how Lil handles things day after day. And the way she talks to Amy as if she can really hear her."

Gladys said, "I tell you that young lady is somethin'. The first couple of days after they brought Amy in, she was so stressed out. Her husband couldn't get her to go home, even to change clothes. I was afraid she would have a nervous breakdown.

"And then on the second night she asked me to watch Amy for a little while so she could go to the hospital chapel. She was gone about forty five minutes, and when she came back she smiled, and sat down beside Amy. She took Amy's hand and began to talk to her. I tell you, Lil almost glowed. Her smile seemed to radiate love right into that child.

"When I asked her what had happened. She said, 'I just went and had a talk with Jesus, just like I use to when I was a girl. He always comes when I get serious, and really reach out to him from my heart.'

"Well, ever since that night," Gladys was saying, "Lil has believed that Amy can hear her. So she talks to her just like she was sittin' up in that bed listenin' to every word. She sings her Christian songs and reads her stories. She even tells her what's goin' on at home and at the school. She says she does it so Amy won't get too far behind and she can keep up with what her friends are doin'.

"I'll tell you somethin' for sure, that young woman's faith has sure had an effect on me. I've been goin' back to church and I even changed my schedule so that I could have Sundays off. I've also been readin' my Bible again. I figure if one person can have that kind of faith, then so can I."

Debbie was a little taken back by the way Gladys seemed to defend Lil, but she was also curious to understand. What had happened that night in the prayer chapel? What could cause such a change? She could sure use some of that kind of strength.

That same evening after Lil and Peter had gone to bed. Peter turned toward Lil and said, "Could I talk to you about something?"

Lil cocked her head to one side; there was just something about the way Peter asked the question. "Of course, you can talk to me about anything, you know that."

"Remember in the hospital the other day when I woke you from dreaming about Amy? You told me that it was a blessing and not just luck that you were able to see Amy in your dreams."

"Yes, I remember and you told me that you wished you could see her in your dreams."

"That's right, and you suggested that I pray and ask God that I might be able to see Amy in my own dreams. Well, I did pray."

"Oh Peter, tell me what happened. Have you seen her?" Lil was so excited she could hardly stand it.

Peter smiled and said, "Yes, I have seen her. I wasn't able to talk to her like you do, but I could see her and I could tell that she could see me too. She smiled and waved at me, and she had a book that she held up for me to see. It was a children's book. I couldn't read what it said, but it had a picture of a garden on it."

Lil was about to burst, she was so excited by now. Lil thought, God is giving us a confirmation. I never doubted any of it, but what a blessing for Peter and for me. Now we have both seen the garden. Thank you, Jesus.

Lil had almost forgotten poor Peter. He was sitting up in bed and grinning from ear to ear. "The book," he said "It's the one you've been reading in your dreams, right?"

"Yes Peter, I believe it is." They both started laughing and thanking God. Because they knew that Amy was alright, and that she would be coming home. Their God would see to it.

Chapter Two

The next day, Lil was sitting by Amy and reading her a story when she heard a tap on the door. She looked up to see Debra. Deb stepped into the room and said, "I hope I'm not interrupting anything, but could I ask you a few questions?"

Lil shook her head and said, "No you're not interrupting. Besides, Amy probably knows this story by heart anyway. Tell me, what can I help you with?"

"You know Lil, I hardly know where to start, but one thing I've wondered about is the way you talk to Amy. It's almost like you expect her to answer you."

Lil thought for a minute. This was the door Lil had been hoping would open. She didn't want what she said to seem frivolous. "I guess in a way I am expecting Amy to answer. I just don't know when that will be. You see Debra, by the second night Amy was here, I realized that I was not walking in faith at all. In fact I would have to say that I was almost paralyzed by fear. I think if I hadn't dealt with the fear, it would have eventually made me sick."

Debbie nodded at that. She could sure identify with that kind of fear, and then she said, "I hope you don't mind but I asked Gladys about you and your faith just last night. She told me that you had suddenly changed, right after you had gone into the little chapel. I have been really curious to ask you what happened. What did you do to make such a difference?"

Lil couldn't help but smile as she remembered that night. She had been so tired, but she was afraid to let herself relax, even a little bit. It was as if she felt that she was the only thing that was keeping Amy connected to this life.

She told Debbie, "I was literally afraid to go to sleep. After all, I had to hold things together for Amy's sake, but then I finally realized that I simply could not do this alone. So I made my way to the chapel to do what I should have done at the very beginning. I got done on my knees and asked the Lord to help me. Of course, I had already prayed from the very first second that I heard the news about Amy, but I also knew that I hadn't even begun to trust God."

Then Lil added, "This is the part that always seems to be the hardest. Perhaps you've heard the saying *(Let go and let God.)* To be honest, I'm sure most Christian would have to admit to a little doubt here and there. The problem seems to be in figuring out which part is God's part and which part is ours. At least I seem to have the need to be in control. I always need to be doing something."

Lil paused, "Well Debbie, that night I knew that I had to give my burden to the Lord, so I could do my part and take care of myself and my family.

"There is a scripture that says, 1 Peter 5:7 *(Casting all your anxiety upon Him, for He cares for you.)* I did the very thing I have been doing for as long as I can remember. I got down on my knees and began to talk with Jesus. I knew that He already understood exactly what was going on. So I admitted that I was afraid, and I asked the Lord to give me strength and to please, watch over Amy.

"After a while I became quiet as the Lord brought scriptures to my mind. I began to feel the trust again and the hope in my heart that Amy would come back to us. Jesus let me know that He was there with her, and also that we needed to talk to her. By talking to her we let her know that we would never give up on her. Plus we would show our faith that we knew her spirit was still here and we would be her anchor."

Lil looked up and smiled, as she said, "So Debbie, when you ask me what I did to make such a difference I would have to say I surrendered. I gave up the control to God."

Debbie just sat there for a while not saying anything. In fact she was so quiet that Lil began to wonder if she had offended her.

Debra finally looked Lil right in the eyes and said, "I don't want to hurt your feelings Lil, but you have been a believer all your life. David and I are just not sure what we believe. I guess

I believe that there has to be a God, but I've never been sure that he cares about me or that he would ever listen to me if I did try and pray to him. He just seems so distant."

Lil was about to comment when she realized that David had been standing in the doorway.

"I'm sorry," he said, "I didn't mean to eavesdrop, but I just got caught up in what you were telling Debbie. Wow, I just can't grasp the idea of having a talk with Jesus. I guess I'm with Deb. God has never seemed that accessible to me. But I must admit that it is obvious that you and Peter have something that I haven't noticed in that many people. You sort of project something. I'm not even sure what to call it. Joy or peace maybe, yeah, I think that's it. You have a peace about you."

Debbie said, "Yes, I've noticed that too. It was hard for me to be around you at first. I just couldn't understand how you could be so positive all the time with your daughter lying here in a coma. Then after a while I became aware that it wasn't just a face you put on. But what you have was coming from the inside."

"Yes," David agreed, "I guess you could say it's not just how you act, but it is who you are.".

"I do appreciate what you are saying, but I also must to tell you that it truly isn't us. What you're seeing comes from our relationship with Jesus. Without that, we would be just as overcome with the cares and fears of the world as anyone else."

"Well," David said, "Maybe someday you can show us how we can get from where we are, to where you are, because right now we are very frightened and basically clueless."

Lil nodded and said, "I think you are in just the right place to begin your search for God. I would guess that most people, even many of those who have been raised in the church, probably come to the Lord during a crisis. I would like to suggest that you get a Bible and start reading in the New Testament. I like the gospel of John. In fact I'm pretty sure I have a gospel of John in my purse. Would you accept it from me as your first step to a better life?"

David and Debbie were in agreement that they could use all the help they could get. Lil got the gospel from her purse and gave it to them. "There is one scripture I would like to share with you if I may. It's actually in the Old Testament, but it's a perfect fit for where you're at right now. It is Jeremiah 29:13. *It reads, (And you will seek Me and find Me, when you search for Me with all of your heart.)* Remember Debbie? I talked about God's part and our part. Well this is your part for right now, to just seek Him."

When Lil got home she shared with Peter about what had happened at the hospital. About how all of a sudden the door seems to be opening to reach out to Debbie and David.

"That is wonderful news," Peter smiled, "You know Lil; sometimes I'm even amazed at your faith. I know you said that they have seen this peace in both of us, but you are the rock. You may lose focus every now and then, but never for very long."

"Thank you Peter, but wasn't I the one that was afraid to fall sleep and kept trying to control everything? I'm not so sure it wasn't pure exhaustion rather than faith that brought me to my knees that time, but thank the Lord; He doesn't give up on us."

Across town there was some pretty serious reading going on at the Miller's house. David looked up at his wife, as she sat reading from their home Bible. He had been reading from the gospel of John that Lil had given them.

He finally said, "You know I'm sure I've read or at least heard some of this before, but after talking with Lil it just seems to have more meaning. I just know there is something here and I *need* to find it. I am going to have to make a list of questions to ask Lil. I wonder, do you think Peter would be willing to talk to me about this? I've already got so many questions, like right here it talks about being born again, but what exactly does that mean?"

Deb was so wrapped up in her own study that it took her a minute to focus on what David was saying to her. "I'm sure that Peter would be happy to talk with you. And I know what you mean about it seeming different. I suppose it's because we have such a pressing need right now and let's face it, we definitely need some answers. But come here a minute honey, I want you to see this. I have been reading this over and over and it's just amazing how it speaks to our situation."

David got up to see what Deb had found and he was surprised to see that she was reading in Jeremiah 29. "Look" she said, pointing to a place in the Bible, "Remember that scripture that Lil gave us? Well I decided to look it up just to see how it reads in our Bible. She gave us verse 13 about seeking God with your heart, but look at verses 11 and 12 (*For I know the plans I have for you, declares the Lord, plans for welfare and not for calamity, to give you a future and a hope. Then you will call upon Me and come and pray to Me, I will listen to you.*) And then it goes on into verse 13 about seeking."

"Wow Deb, you are right. That is so powerful. It's almost like He is speaking directly to us." David took hold of Debbie's shoulders and pulled her up from the table.

"What do you think Deb? I believe that I'm ready to pray for our little girl. Where do you think we should go?"

Debbie took David's hand and said, "I don't think *where* is all that important. Let's just kneel right here and reach out from our hearts like it says."

So right there in the dining room they knelt down and asked the Lord to help them in their search and to please be with Melisa. "Lord", cried Debbie, "We are so new at this, but the Bible tells us that you would listen. So Lord, help us to learn to trust in you and please be with Melisa. Let us know if there's anything we can do to help her."

David cried out too, "God help us to trust you and to have the kind of faith that we see in the Iversons. And Lord I feel I need to ask you to forgive me for not coming to you sooner." When they finished, Debbie went into David's arms and they both shed a few tears, but somehow they knew that things had changed that night.

Chapter Three

Lil was aware that Peter had gotten up early to go to his weekly staff meeting. He bent over and kissed her goodbye, "Sweet dreams," he said. And then all was quite again.

It seemed like just a few moments and I found myself in the garden again . . . .

What a very special place this is with bees buzzing and the birds singing. I held the book in my hands but I wasn't reading right then.

Earlier I had read about an ant colony, about what hard workers they are, and how sometimes as many as a dozen or more ants will work together to bring one morsel of food back to the colony. They are very industrious, not so different from a city where people work together toward a specific goal. I thought to myself, better to be an ant than a sluggard . . . .

I was still thinking on this when I heard the sound of laughter coming from some bushes. I got up to investigate and became aware of some children off in the distance. I was about to turn back to the bench I had been sitting on when Amy jumped out in front of me. "Did I scare you Mommy?"

"No dear, you did surprise me, but I don't think it is possible to feel fear here."

Amy thought a little before she answered, "I guess you're right, at least mostly. I know when I woke up here . . . . I wasn't afraid. But remember the little girl I told you about, Melisa? She was sort of afraid when she first came here."

"Yes", I answered, "I do remember you telling me about her. I hope she is doing better. You do know, don't you that Melisa is in the hospital? In fact she is in the room right next door to you?"

"Yes Mommy, I know that her body is at the hospital, but here in the garden she is doing much better. Ever since she got to see Jesus, she wasn't afraid anymore."

This was said as if it was the most normal thing in the world. "And Mommy, I got to see Daddy for a little while. I hope he can come again." . . . .

Amy's words faded away as Lil suddenly woke up. She was back in her bedroom.

Amy had told Lil before that she had gotten to see Jesus. She thought to herself, what a lovely thing for the Lord to do, to allow these little ones to see Him. Perhaps she would tell Debbie about what Amy said about Missy.

"What do you think I should do Lord? I believe it would bless her, but it might be hard for her to hear how I 'm able to see my daughter in dreams. Please give me wisdom Lord."

When Lil arrived at the hospital Debbie was already there and she gave Lil a great big smile. She rushed over to Lil and began talking so fast, Lil had to get her to sit down and start over.

She was shaking her head and saying, "I have so much to tell you. The first and most important thing would be to tell you that David and I got down on our knees and prayed for Missy last night. I think it's the first time we've ever done that, not just for Missy but I'm sure we have never prayed together before."

"Well, tell me how did it feel?" Lil asked.

Debbie continued, "I don't know if I can express it. It felt good but it also felt kind of strange. Well not exactly strange, but different, sort of foreign. Does that make any sense?"

Lil nodded and said, "I think it is bound to feel different, after all this is a whole new world for you. But tell me more. You seem so happy. I want details, Okay?"

Debra smiled, and then went on, "When David and I got home I decided to get out the Bible we have. I'm not sure where we got it, but any way I wanted to look up the scripture you quoted from Jeremiah. And then while I was there I just read a little above it and I was amazed at how it spoke right to our needs. *(It talks about God's plans for us, to give us a future and hope.* And it said that He would hear us when we pray.) David had been reading the gospel you gave him and we both felt as if, what we were reading was speaking directly to us. Can you imagine that?"

Lil was happy to hear what Debbie was saying and made the comment, "It sounds like you are doing your part and God is speaking to you through the scriptures. It doesn't really surprise me. I don't know how many times I have heard people say that exact same thing, about it seeming like a verse of scripture is speaking right to them. That is the way that God speaks to us most of the time. That's why it is so important to spend time reading God's word and also spending time in prayer. It's so neat what you found there. So you see, by His revealing that to you, I get blessed as well."

Lil got up and gave Debbie a big hug and then they went together to see their daughters . . . . While they were sitting in Melisa's room, Debbie looked up, as she took her daughter's hand and said, "I think I need to start talking to Missy the way you talk to Amy."

Lil nodded her agreement. Debbie went on, "I also have been meaning to ask you about something I overheard the nurses talking about. I've heard them say that you have dreams where you have been able to see Amy."

Debbie paused and then asked, "Is that true? Have you had dreams? And can you tell me what you saw? Are you able to talk to Amy or just see her?" The questions just came tumbling out and Debbie began to cry.

Lil sat down on the bed next to Deb and put her arm around her. "It's alright Debbie." She said, "You can ask me anything. And yes, I have been able to see Amy in dreams. In fact, I had a dream this morning just before I woke up. And I have been praying about whether or not I should share it with you, because in this dream I actually talked to Amy about Melisa."

"Oh yes please tell me anything. What did she say about Missy? Please, anything at all."

16

"Okay," Lil said, "But first let me tell you a little about how this blessing came to be. About a month after Amy went into her coma, I got pretty discouraged. Even though I had God's promises, I asked Him to please give me some kind of assurance. I didn't know what to expect. I just knew there would be something.

"It was few nights later when I had the first dream, in which Amy came to me and said, *'Mommy, don't worry I'm okay. I'm here in a garden and I got to talk to Jesus. He's really nice Mommy and there are other children here too.'*

"I woke up way too quickly, but I knew the Lord had blessed me and I began to praise Him for giving me the assurance I needed."

Then Debbie looked up with tears and said, "Please tell me what Amy said about Missy. Is she in the garden too?"

Lil wanted to remember the exact words that Amy said about Melisa. She closed her eyes so she could concentrate for a minute before she told Debbie, "Amy first mentioned Melisa the first night she was here, but not by name. Then the next day she talked about her again and said her name is Melisa."

Debbie sat up a little straighter and said, "She called her Melisa? Had you told her what her name was?"

"No Debbie, I hadn't told her. And then she told me that at first Melisa was just a little bit afraid, until she talked with Jesus."

"Oh," Debbie cried, "She's okay then, right? My baby's okay, if she's with Jesus."

Lil put her arm around Debbie and said, "I'm sure she is okay and I believe she is lovingly cared for. That's what I sensed about Amy once I was able to see her. I knew the Lord was with her, and that perhaps there were angels watching over her. I also became aware that she knew what was going on here in the hospital."

Lil paused and then went on, "There is one other thing that Amy said about Melisa. When I asked her if she knew that Melisa was here in the hospital, she said something that surprised me. Her exact words were, *'Yes, I know that her body* *is at the hospital, but <u>here</u> in the garden she is doing much better, ever since she got to see Jesus'."*

Lil stood up and turned to face Debbie and added, "That says to me that what we see in the natural is definitely not all there is. I believe the Lord is saying we are to trust, even though what we are seeing in the natural is scary. We are not to focus on the natural, but on the things which we cannot see. There is a scripture that lines up with this perfectly. It is 2 Cor. 5:7 *(for we walk by faith, not by sight.)* I believe we are to focus on what God is doing in the spirit."

Lil went on, "Debbie there is so much about the spiritual side of things that we just don't comprehend. There are a couple of scriptures I would like to show you, if that would be okay."

Debbie nodded, and answered, "Sure that would be fine. It is just so hard to grasp all of this but I do appreciate your telling me about what Amy had to say about Missy. It truly has encouraged me."

Lil went into her daughter's room to get her Bible, and when she came back into Melisa's room she heard Debbie talking to Missy, telling her that she and her daddy were doing everything they could to bring her back to them. Lil waited for a few minutes to give her time to draw closer to her child and to God, and then she went over and sat down and looked up the scriptures that she felt certain the Lord was leading her to show Debra.

"Okay, here are the scriptures I feel the Lord wants me to share with you."

Debbie just shook her head and said, "You see, even that is amazing to me that God cares enough about me, to give you scriptures to help me. But I am so glad that He does."

Lil laughed and then said, "You ain't seen nothing yet." That got a smile out of Debbie.

"The first scripture is Proverbs 3:5 *(Trust in the LORD with all your heart, And do not lean on your own understanding.)*

"And here is another one from Ephesians 3:20, *(Now to Him who is able to do exceeding abundantly beyond all that we ask or think, according to the power that works within us.)*

"You see Debbie, we can't begin to understand all that is going on here, but we can be sure that God is aware of our needs and is doing whatever He can to comfort us."

Lil closed her Bible and asked, "Well Debbie, what do you think about what I just read?"

She looked up with a very somber expression on her face and said, "I think we can trust Him!"

But Lil saw the gleam in her eye and then they both laughed. Then Lil added, "Absolutely! You can count on it."

Chapter Four

That evening as Lil cleaned up after their dinner, the conversation she'd had with Debbie kept going around in her head. Lil wondered to herself. Did I say the right things? Did I give her the right scriptures? She felt confident that she was following God's direction. She truly felt that God was using her to reach out to Debbie. As she remembered she found herself tickled at what Debbie had said about trusting God. She had seen the sparkle in her eye, but she knew that Deb was taking the scriptures very seriously. In fact Deb had written all the scriptures down so she could look them up at home.

Lil finished up in the kitchen and went looking for Peter to tell him about her day. She found him in his home office going over some contracts. As always he looked up with a smile, not minding the intrusion.

"Hey", he said, "What's up? You seem pleased about something, I heard you singing in the kitchen."

Lil stepped into the room and said, "Have you got a minute? There is something I would like to share with you, and yes, I am pleased."

Peter patted the chair next to his desk and said, "For you, I've always got time. Now, what has put that lovely smile on your face?"

Lil sat down and began to share with him about her conversation with Debbie and how she was being stirred up about the scriptures. She said, "I think she is starting to trust in what the Bible says."

Peter smiled and said, "That is great news. Tell me more about what happened."

And so Lil told him all she could remember about her discussion with Debbie. "So that's why I am grinning so much."

Peter raised his eyebrows and said, "I am so happy to hear that Debbie is coming around. I wasn't sure that she would because she was so closed at the beginning."

Lil responded by saying, "I think she was just hurting so much and was looking for someone to blame."

"I'm sure you are right, you're just more sensitive than I am. Now are you ready to hear my good news?"

"I am ready and it's only fair. So fire away. Tell me about your day."

"First of all, I got a phone call from David asking me out to lunch so that we could talk about some of the things he has read in the gospel of John that you gave him."

"Oh Peter," Lil said, "Surely the Lord is in this."

"I believe He is." Peter responded, "David wanted to know about what being born again was all about. So I explained a little about what it means to experience the New Birth. I also told him how man was given free will in the garden and then how they fell. I showed him how the curse came into the world because of Adam's sin. And how the devil became god of this world. I explained that the devil is the one who is out to hurt us. God doesn't cause these bad things to happen, but He does show us the way back."

Peter took a breath and then added, "That's about all we were able to cover on our lunch hour. What do think? Did I steer him right? You know I'm not very good at this."

Lil said, "My goodness Peter, I think you did great and I am very impressed. I didn't know you could preach!"

He shook his head and said, "Yeah right, you're the preacher in our family."

"I don't know," Lil mused, "I think you're giving me some competition."

They had a bit of a laugh and then they got serious again. Lil and Peter spent some time in prayer for Amy and Melisa. They also held up David and Debbie. They asked the Lord for a break through, for both families.

After a while they headed up to bed. Peter kissed his wife and said something that he often said now, "Sweet dreams."

Lil responded, "And I wish you the same Peter."

They both had the scriptures and the conversations from their day rolling around in their heads. But before falling asleep they had both offered up one more prayer from their hearts. Thanking God for His many blessings.

I found myself sitting under a lovely tree in the garden. I held the book in my hand and for the first time I was able to read the title of the book.

The book was titled, *"The Garden of Blessings"*. Yes, I thought, that does fit. I have certainly been blessed by this wonderful place. I began to read the next chapter.

(Toby was very interested in a little green frog that would jump just as he was about to pounce. He didn't want to harm the frog, because in this garden everything was good. No one ever got hurt. There were only good things here, only blessings. His mistress called out, "Toby what are you doing? Are you teasing that frog again?"

No thought Toby, I'm just playing. I kind of like showing off just a little bit, cause I can jump so high. The little girl came over and picked Toby up and then sat down on the grass to pet him. "You know Toby your full name is Tobias and in Hebrew that name means, 'God is good'. So you have to be good too." Toby thought, well that's kind of silly because everything in this garden is already good.)

I looked up from my reading because I became aware of happy voices talking and singing. And I could see many children. They were singing a very familiar song. "Yes, Jesus loves me, yes, Jesus loves me, yes, Jesus loves me, for the Bible tells me so." I thought to myself, thank you so much Jesus, for loving the little children.

Suddenly the children took off running. I was about to try and stop one of them to ask what was going on when Amy appeared and said, "Hello Mommy." And then she reached out and touched me with the tips of her fingers. This had never happened before. I'm not sure why, it just seemed like some unspoken rule. But now when she put her fingers on my arm I just felt this enormous peace go through me. She looked at me so sweetly. I wasn't sure if I should laugh or cry.

Then she said, "This is so good Mommy, because you're just in time to see them loose the blessings." I wasn't sure what to say. In fact I wasn't sure if I could even speak.

I finally pulled myself together enough to ask, "What blessings honey? I don't understand. Why did all the children run off?"

Amy smiled that lovely smile that I could never resist and simply said, "We are in the Garden of Blessings. And every so often when everything is ready, the angels come and get the blessing from the children and take them to the people that need them."

Then Amy turned away and I followed her into an open area where there were many children. They were holding up their arms as if they were handing something to some large and very beautiful beings. I realized these were the angels that Amy was talking about. As soon as each angel received something from one of the children they would turn to leave and then they would simply disappear.

"Oh Amy, I don't understand what is happening, but it's so incredibly awesome."

"I know Mommy. Isn't it beautiful? I have to go now Mommy and give the angel my blessing. I love you and Daddy so much."

I called after her to wait, but she had already disappeared into the crowd of children. I just shouted, "I love you too sweetheart."

Lil woke up slowly. She didn't want to let go of this truly special dream. She thought, Lord they've all been special, but this time Amy touched me. I don't know about the other blessing that went out today, but I do know I received one of them. She got out of bed and got down on her knees to thank the Lord for this wonderful gift.

The following morning Peter said, "You are absolutely glowing. You must have seen Amy in the garden again last night."

Lil was still in a state of absolute euphoria. She nodded and said, "I'm not sure if I can even talk about it. Oh Peter, the dream was so special this time and different. I feel so blessed."

Peter said, "I sure would like to share in that blessing. Can you please try?" Lil asked Peter to pray with her first and thank the Lord for the very special gift He had given to her. Then she went on to share the dream with Amy's father.

Chapter Five

That same morning Lil made her way into the hospital to see her little girl. She almost expected her to be sitting up to greet her but it was only wishful thinking. But she knew that one day it would happen so she would not give up!

About that time Debbie stuck her head in the door and asked, "Am I intruding? I sure have some things that I would like to talk to you about." When Lil looked up she had tears in her eyes and Debbie rushed over to put her arm around her. "What is it? Has something happened?"

Lil shook her head before saying, "No I'm fine. I just got a little emotional. I had a special visit with Amy and it was so real. I actually thought that she just might . . . . Oh I don't know, I think I'm just being foolish. What can I do for you Deb?"

Debbie sat down and said, "No, I think it's my turn to offer you some support. I have often wondered how you have coped all these months. You are always so upbeat and positive. Please tell me if there is anything that I can do."

Lil took Debbie's hand and said, "Oh Deb, it's really not anything bad. It's just that I had another dream last night and it was so real. I guess I honestly hoped to see my daughter smiling up at me when I came in this morning."

"As for how I cope, it has to be my faith and of course the dreams have been a tremendous comfort. But even if I didn't have them I would still believe that somehow Amy will come back to us."

Debbie said, "Can you share the dream with me or is it too personal?"

"Yes, of course I can share it and I believe it will bless you too." Lil told Debbie about the book she read in the garden. And she went on to tell her about the Garden of Blessings and how the children were so involved with the whole process. Then Lil told her how Amy had touched her.

Debbie let out a small gasp when Lil told her about the touch. Lil quickly added, "Thank goodness we can still touch them here and hold them. You know Debbie I truly believe that some of the blessings the children handed to the angels were for us. And I absolutely believe that you and David have a blessing on the way." We both just sat there for a while reflecting on the dream and on the blessings.

After they had talked about the garden, Debbie related to Lil how excited David had been about his conversation with Peter. How he talked about being born of the Spirit. And also what Peter said, about the devil being the god of this world.

Debbie said, "I don't understand how Satan can be god of anything? I'm pretty sure he's the one who does a lot of terrible things. But how can he be called a god? I just don't get it."

So Lil spent some time with Debbie going over the things that Peter had told David. Showing her in the Bible how this all took place. Then she went on to tell her how Jesus came to earth to redeem us.

Finally Debra said, "Is there any hope for David and me?" We aren't like you and Peter and we sure haven't lived our lives for God. We haven't even been going to church. Maybe it's too late for us?"

Lil's quick response was, "No of course it's not too late. It is never too late to get right with God." Lil added, "Besides the word tells us all things are possible with God. But Debbie, you and David will have to make a decision.

Hebrews 11:6 tells us that, (*And without faith it is impossible to please Him, for he who comes to God must believe that He is, and that He is a rewarder of those who seek Him.*)

And then the gospel of John 6:37 says, (*and the one who comes to Me I will certainly not cast out.*) So you see Debbie, it is really up to you and David."

"Right now I feel like we have more of a chance than I ever thought we would. Thanks to you." Debbie answered thoughtfully.

"You know of course, that Peter and I are praying for you. So just think about what we've talked about and feel free to ask us any question you might have."

Then after Debbie had talked with Melisa's doctor she called to tell David that things were about the same. According to the doctor Missy could wake up at any time and not have any lasting damage, or the coma could continue.

David was quiet for a moment before he answered, "I know that I absolutely will not give up hope that she will wake up. We have to hang on to that hope. And Deb I am starting to believe that God does care about us and I believe He heard our prayers the other night. What about you Deb? Do you think that together we can find God?"

"Yes I do, and I am learning more about Him every day. And David, I feel like something special is going on here; it's almost like destiny. Just think about the timing of our meeting Lil and Peter right at the same time Missy slipped into her coma. And what a help they have been to us."

"Yes," said David, "They truly have been an encouragement. They really do understand and I'm sure it's because they have been through this same thing. Deb, can you hold on a second? I think Peter is on the other line."

Deb said, "Sure, go ahead and see what he wants."

After a short time David was back on the line. He said, "Deb that was Peter and he was asking if we would like to go with them to the Wednesday night service at their church. I said that I would check with you. What do you think? Would you like to go?"

Debbie didn't have to think long before she answered. "Yes, David I would like that very much." . . . .

They said their goodbyes and Debbie went looking for Lil. She was starting to believe what Lil had told her. That some of the blessing the children were handing to the angels truly were coming their way.

After finding Lil, Debbie told her about the phone call with David. Then Lil explained a little about what the service at their church would be like. She said they usually sing a few worship songs to help everybody get into a spiritual frame of mind. Next they would hear a short message. Then they would break up into smaller groups and discuss in greater detail what the pastor had taught.

Once they finished talking about the church, Debbie shared with Lil what the doctor had said about how there shouldn't be any permanent damage to Melisa. That is providing she woke up sooner rather than later. Then she said, "Oh Lil, I so want my little girl back just the way she was before. And I am beginning to have some hope that it will happen."

Finally Debbie attempted to ask Lil a question that had been on her mind for quite a while. She paused and reached out to touch Lil's hand and said, "I have been so focused on my own needs that I haven't really thought about what you've been through. I know you have a lot of faith and that you believe Amy will wake up. Lil, I don't even know how to ask you this, but aren't you worried about . . . ." Debbie stopped and hung her head not able to go on.

"I understand what you are trying to say Debbie. And Peter and I are pretty much handling things one day at a time. We already know for Amy to wake up after all this time it would have to be a miracle. So we just go one step farther and believe that our loving Father will bring her back to us whole.

"We are prepared to work with her to gain all of her physical dexterity back. It is possible she will have to relearn some things. She might need help with her speech. That is why I talk to her so much. I know that most doctors are focused on the natural. They feel that a person in a coma can't hear us when we talk to them. However, we believe that they can hear us in the spirit. They may not be able to react in the natural to what we are saying to them. But I still believe they can receive what we say to them into their spirits.

"I have heard many a story about people being aware of what was going on around them during operations. Some even looking down on their own bodies and later relating conversation that they heard. There have also been reports of such stories coming from people who awaken from comas. So I will give medicine every chance while I keep on trusting God to do all the rest."

"Oh Lil, I am so bless to have gotten to know you. Both you and Peter have given us something to hang on to. We are so fortunate that Amy was at this hospital and right next door to Melisa at this exact time."

"Actually, there is even more to this coincidence than you are even aware of. You see Debbie because of the insurance we have had to divide Amy's care between our home and the hospital. We care for her at home most of the time. We have a physical therapist coming in to help with exercising her limbs to keep her muscles from atrophying."

"Oh my goodness I had no idea. I should have realized that she couldn't have been kept here all this time. It just didn't occur to me."

Lil said, "It's alright Debbie. In fact, we brought Amy back in so the doctors could monitor her care for a while. They wanted to make sure there were no infections and to run some tests. She had only been back here for one day when you brought Melisa in. So you see it was even a bigger coincidence that Amy was here at the same time as Missy."

Debbie considered that for a while before saying, "I don't believe in coincidences."

Lil nodded and said, "You know Debbie, neither do I." The two mothers nodded in agreement and then embraced one another.

Chapter Six

On Wednesday evening as the Millers got ready for church Debra said, "A few weeks ago I would not have believed we would be going to a church service. Now I am actually looking forward to it. How do you feel about all of this David?"

He answered, "I know what you mean and I wouldn't have believed it either. But I am excited and ready to learn more, even though I am a little apprehensive. I do appreciate that Lil told you a little about the service. This way we know what to expect. You know Deb, we haven't been to church since we tried going right after we were first married. I guess we were searching for something even back then."

"You're right," Debbie said, "We just didn't know what it was that we were searching for. Now I know that I would like to have the kind of peace and faith that Lil and Peter have."

At about six thirty the Iversons picked up Debra and David and drove them to the church. The service went just about the way that Lil had described it. Right at first they were both a little nervous but it didn't take long until the other church members made them feel right at home.

"Wow," said David, "This is so different from my past experience with church. Not near as somber and everyone is so warm and friendly. I actually feel welcome."

Peter smiled and said, "It's important to find a church that you're comfortable in. It's also very important to find a church that preaches Jesus, from the Word of God. What is taught must be backed up by the Bible. That way you can relax and trust what you're receiving."

The rest of the evening went forward about the way they expected. David and Debra enjoyed the music. They did mostly choruses making it easier to learn.

Then the Pastor gave his message. The Millers were surprised when he began to speak on, "God's Blessings" with the key passage taken from Gal 3. But it didn't seem to surprise Lil and Peter at all. After the lesson they broke up into smaller groups and the Millers met some very nice people. Both David and Debbie were impressed by the lively discussion that went on in the study group. And there were so many scriptures that talked about the blessings of God.

The study lasted about 30 minutes. Then they took some time to pray for one another's needs before they all went home . . . .

On the way home Debbie and David were very quiet as they thought over what they had just experienced. They had been prepared to leave if they felt uncomfortable, which they never did. Instead they had experienced the warmth of the congregation. The whole evening had been a pleasant surprise.

When Peter pulled into the Miller's drive way, both David and Debbie started talking at once. Then they laughed.

Peter said, "For a minute there I thought the two of you had lost your ability to speak. I'm glad you have recovered."

David spoke up, "I think we were both just mulling over the service. The music and the study were so different from what either of us ever experienced before. We are happy that we went with you tonight and it has certainly given us a lot to think about. Thank you for inviting us."

They headed for the front door and Debbie turned and called to Lil, "See you in the morning."

The next morning as Lil parked she was reflecting on the evening before. She thought how wonderful it is to have a God that you can depend on. She knew Debra and David had been surprised to hear that the message was on God's blessings. It was a subject that was on all of their minds because of the dreams that Lil had shared with them. She had seen this happen so many times, where the Lord would reach out to meet someone right where they were. Lil thanked the heavenly Father for His loving kindness.

When she got inside she was greeted by a beaming Gladys. Gladys grabbed her in a giant bear hug. Lil hugged back. What else could she do? Then after, Lil was able to get her breath again she asks Gladys, "What in the world brought that on?"

"Oh my goodness," answered Gladys, "I hardly know where to start. It's about my son and those blessins' you've been passin' around. Oh I think I need to sit down." . . . . And Gladys did just that, but she was still grinning from ear to ear.

"Well," Lil prompted, "Tell me what all the smiles are about? Please!"

And so Gladys explained. "For starters, I've been expectin' a blessin' ever since you told me about that dream and about all those little children handin' those blessins' to the angels. Well, I got me a humdinger of a blessin'."

"Go on." Lil encouraged.

Gladys continued, "I must say, I am almost speechless. Lil, I'm pretty sure I told you a while back that my nineteen year old son just up and took off about a year ago. All he left was a note sayin' not to worry. Like that was goin' a happen.

"Well to make a long story short, he came home a couple of days ago. He said that his new girlfriend had told him if he wanted a relationship with her, then he would have to make things right with his mama and with God. I didn't think it could get any better than that and then last night he went to church with me and rededicated his life to the Lord."

Lil was impressed and very happy. Gladys however wasn't quite through. She went on, "Now, how's that for a blessin' from the good Lord? I knew when you were talkin' about those blessins' that I was goin a grab one for myself."

Finally Lil got a chance to tell Gladys just how happy she was to hear her wonderful news. Lil had been so pleased when Gladys had told her that she had started back to church shortly after they had met. Gladys had always been so good with Amy. She was very loving and patient with her. She also talked to her just like Lil did.

When Lil looked up she realized that Debbie had been standing there and had heard the wonderful news. In fact,

Debbie went over to Gladys and gave her a big hug. Then she said, "That is great news! I'm so happy for you Gladys."

After one more hug from everyone Gladys said, "Thank you all for prayin' for me, especially you Lil. I can't tell you how glad I am that I met you." Then she headed back to work with a bit of a glow all around her.

Lil took Debbie by the arm and led her into Amy's room before she said, "Didn't I tell you, 'That you ain't seen nothing yet'?"

Debbie grinned and said, "You absolutely did tell me that and now I have a lot more questions to ask you. And I need to know if you're ready?"

"You bet," Lil answered, "I figured you would have a few questions after last night. And I want to know what you thought of the service? Did you like it?"

"Lil, I can't begin to tell you how good it felt to be a part of something that you know in your heart to be the truth. David and I talked way into the night. We figured that we wouldn't get a lot of sleep anyway, so we just kept going over what we learned. It really helped having the study guide they handed out giving us a summary of the sermon.

"I guess you can see that I'm really fired up but you should see David. I have never seen him like this except maybe when Melisa was born. And Melisa is the reason we started searching. I only wish we could have seen all these things sooner."

Lil took her hand and said, "Remember Debbie, just a few days ago you were asking me if it was too late for you and David. Peter and I believe the Lord is always, right on time. And we are going to pray all the way through to His promise of healing for our daughters. Because I believe that's what the Lord wants for them."

At the same time across town David stopped in to see Peter at his office. Peter looked up from his desk, surprised to see David approaching. He stood up to shake David's hand and said, "Hello David, I didn't expect to see you here. Are you looking to purchase a house?"

"No," responded David, "But I am looking for some answers, and I'm hoping you have a few minutes. I was going to call you for lunch again, but I was already in the area to go to the library. So I took a chance and stopped by now."

Peter came around the desk, motioned to a room off to his left and said, "Of course, I can take a few minutes. What's on your mind, David?"

David followed Peter into the room. It was a small room with a desk and three chairs. It was most likely used to write up contracts. Instead of taking a seat behind the desk, Peter sat down in one of the client chairs. Then he motioned for David to take the other one.

David sat down and began asking questions about last night's service. He wanted to know about the key passage of scripture used in the message the night before. The scripture found in Gal.3, about the blessing of Abraham coming on the gentiles through faith. And also, it talked about receiving the promise.

David asked, "How can we receive a promise from the old testament? I don't get it."

Peter took his New Testament from his pocket and opened it to Galatians. He showed him how the promise was made to Abraham and to his seed. And how the blessing was passed down through the generations, until the seed, who was Christ had come.

Peter told him we were kept under the law because of sin, until faith came through Jesus Christ. Finally Peter read, "In *Gal.3:26*, it tells us, *(For you are all sons of God through faith in Christ Jesus.)*"

Then he handed the New Testament to David and had him read on through *Gal.3:27-29*. David read slowly, mulling over each verse carefully.

When he looked up he finally said, "Why haven't I heard this before? I've been to church. In fact Debbie and I tried several churches right after we were married. I never once heard it preached that we could be baptized into Christ. Wow, this is just so incredible. Now that's what I call a blessing, to be baptized into Christ . . . . And speaking of blessings there's you and Lil. Peter, I can't begin to tell you how much help you have given us." He paused and shook his head before he continued, "I came here with a lot of questions. The answers you have given me are simply amazing. I'm sure I will be back with more questions. Right now, I can't wait to tell Deb and share with her what you've showed me today."

Peter rose from his chair and clasped David's hand and said, "You are a good listener David and God can be found, if you are serious and . . . ."

"And you search for Him with all of your heart." Chimed in David, "That was my first lesson, quoted by your lovely wife to Deb and me."

Peter nodded and said, "That doesn't surprise me, she is the rock in our family. Lil has so much faith and she is filled with the Spirit in a way that I haven't begun to comprehend."

Peter walked David out to the front office and said, "We will definitely talk more soon. David I want you to know that you and Debbie have also been a blessing to Lil and me. You have helped us to take the focus off of our own problems. And we've been able to share some of what we have learned in the past few years. It's been good for us to share our faith. I'm sure you know that we're praying for the two of you and for Melisa."

They shook hands again before saying goodbye. Both were eager to share with their spouses what they had talked about. They also felt the Lord's presence in their hearts as they went about the rest of their day. In fact Peter was humming the song, "I'm so very happy Lord, so very happy Lord. I'm so happy, because you're living in my heart today." . . . .

After David saw Peter at his office, he went back to the library. He had been doing a search for a very special book. Up until this morning he hadn't had much luck. But this one lady at the library told him about a web site called (lost pages) where he could search out old books, that are out of print. And since he was trying to keep this search a secret for the time being, he didn't want to use the computers at work or the one at home. So he went back to the library to use one of theirs.

Once he settled in and found the site the librarian had told him about, David discovered that according to the site such a book, by the title he was looking for actually existed. David was stunned . . . . When he had started his search he truly did not expect to find anything.

David sat looking at the screen, which showed the title of the book, supposedly written in 1909. David shook his head and thought to himself, (This can't be the same book.) There was very little information given other than the author's name, Clarence Cook and the year published.

Then upon reading the comments, by others who had visited the site, he read an email by a lady that said she was familiar with this book and had read it when she was a girl. She gave her email address. So David wrote her an email asking her for more information. He gave her his cell phone number in hopes that she would contact him directly. He figured that he would ask her a few question and discover that they were talking about two different books. David headed back to work and pretty much forgot all about his search.

It didn't really surprise Peter to get a call that evening from David, asking if he and Debbie could please come over for a while. After his talk with David that morning he recognized the symptoms of a young man stirred up and on fire concerning the things of the Lord. As David and Debra began searching, they had started to receive revelation from the scriptures.

Peter remembered when he first came to the Lord as a young man of only sixteen. He just couldn't get enough of the Word of God to satisfy his need. He understood now, that what he had experienced was a *(hunger and a thirst for righteousness)*. That was exactly what was happening to David.

During their dinner earlier Lil had told him about her day at the hospital and about the wonderful news Gladys had told them.

Peter said, "Gladys is quite the character. She sure has been taking her relationship with the Lord seriously, ever since you had that encounter with Jesus in the chapel. Gladys is such a good person and she has been like a grandmother to Amy. I sure hope her son is serious about his rededication."

"Yes I know," answered Lil, "She deserves some blessings. It really did tickle me the way she latched onto that dream about the blessing. She was bound and determined to get a hold of one of those blessins' as she called them. She's a real sweet heart. I do think I need to straighten her out about what she said though because she was saying that I was passing out the blessings."

"I wouldn't worry Lil. I'm sure she knows that the blessings are from the Lord. She's just saying that because you're the one who had the dream. And she is feeling so thankful that she got to know you. I can certainly understand that feeling." Peter said this as he leaned over and gave his wife a big kiss.

Lil actually blushed, a little. She was about to scold Peter when the doorbell rang. "We'll talk about this later." She said, as she got up to answer the door.

They welcomed the Millers into their home. Once they got the polite greetings out of the way, David didn't waste any time before he said, "Peter and Lil, thank you so much for seeing us like this. I have to tell you that Deb and I are so excited, ever since you showed me those scriptures in Gal. 3. Especially Gal 3:27, about being baptized into Christ. We want to know is that the new birth?"

Lil and Peter nodded. Then Lil suggested they go into the kitchen where they could sit around the table and do some digging in the scriptures. Lil was pleased to see that Debbie had brought her Bible with her. "First of all," Lil said, "I think we should start with a prayer."

They all held hands and Peter led them in a prayer. "Father, we ask you to bless this time of study. We ask for your wisdom as Lil and I share our faith with our friends. Above all Lord we ask you to join us and make your presence known. In Jesus Name, Amen."

Then Peter said, "To answer your first question, about Gal.3:27. I think it would help you if you read Gal. 3:26, 27 together *(For ye are all sons of God through faith in Christ Jesus. For all of you who were baptized into Christ have clothed yourselves with Christ.)* To be baptized into Christ is actually a result of the New Birth. When you receive Christ into your hearts by faith, you become a child of God. And at the same time you are baptized into the body of Christ by the Holy Spirit."

Lil spoke up and added, "Another good scripture is John 1:12." Lil had already turned to John in her Bible so she handed it to David and then she helped Debbie find it so they could read it together.

David began to read, *"(But as many as received Him, to them He gave the right to become children of God, even to those who believe in His name.)* This is all so powerful and yet really simple. Why has it seemed so hard before?"

"Perhaps it just seems simple now, because your hearts are open to the truth." Lil went on, "The Lord is always aware when the heart turns toward Him and when we search for Him he can be found."

"Yes." David said, "When you search for Him with all of your heart. That seems to have become our scripture."

Debra nodded in agreement. "It sure has!"

After going through a few more scriptures David said, "Is it too soon for Deb and me to make a commitment? I know that I'm ready." He turned to his wife and asked, "How do you feel Deb? I don't want to push you into anything that you're not ready for."

Deb replied, "Yes, I'm ready. I just keep wishing that we would have understood all this sooner."

Lil spoke up, "I wouldn't worry. Just remember what I said, that the Lord is always right on time. Your both ready now and that is what's important. What do you say Peter? I think they understand enough to make a commitment."

"I agree." said Peter, "If you're ready then, Lil and I will lead you in a simple pray of repentance. Then we will give you the opportunity to accept Jesus as your Lord and Savior . . . ."

After they finished the prayer, Debbie and David looked up with tears in their eyes. Then there were hugs all around and since it was getting late they said their goodbyes and headed home.

After the Millers were gone, Lil and Peter thanked and praised the Lord for His precious anointing. As they headed up to bed Peter put his arm around Lil and said, "I believe we have some unfinished business."

Lil just shook her head and then responded by hugging Peter back and saying, "You are incorrigible, but I still love you."

The Millers woke up on Friday morning feeling as if something truly remarkable had happened to them. While they prepared breakfast they were playing an old CD the Iversons had given them. Lil told them it was old but it still has a powerful anointing. There was one song in particular that Debbie really liked. *(I'll keep my heart upon you Lord, I'll keep my heart upon you, Lord I'll pray every day, so I won't lose my way and I'll keep my heart upon you.)* Deb was singing along with the CD in her beautiful soprano voice. "I just love that song." she said, as she continued to sing, her lovely voice filling the kitchen.

"I love to hear you sing. And now with you singing that beautiful song, I may just float to work."

David was a teacher at the Middle School. He liked his job a lot and his students really liked him. They were all being very supportive, about what he was going through right now. They were on their best behavior, but to David it felt like they were walking on egg shells when he was around them. And he would much prefer that things just get back to normal. David wanted his daughter back home.

With tears in his eyes David took a hold of his wife and just held her for a minute before he said, "Deb, I want to pray, really pray for Missy to come home. I want her to be her sweet self again."

Debbie nodded. They sat down at the table and began to lift up their daughter. "Oh dear Father, first of all we thank you so much that we are a part of the body of Christ. Thank you for receiving us and now Dear Lord please, be with Missy and bring her back to us. Lord we want Missy home, with her sweet and lovely spirit as she has always been. Thank you Father and thank you dear Jesus, Amen."

Both Debbie and David wept tears for their daughter. They were quiet as they ate their breakfast and got ready for the rest of their day. After breakfast David kissed Debbie goodbye and then headed to work.

When David got out to the car he saw that he had a voice mail. The message was, "Hello Mr. Miller, what a surprise to hear of someone showing interest in the book, *"The Garden of Blessings"*. Yes, I will be happy to discuss the book with you. My name is Annabelle Towns and I look forward to hearing from you."

David was thrilled but he still wasn't convinced that he had the right book. It was silly to think that there really was a book like the one Lil read in heaven. Wasn't it? "Oh well, I've come this far. I may as well follow this through to the end." He dialed the number but there was no answer and no answering machine. "Well," David thought, "Perhaps Annabelle, is having a little fun with me." David tried again, but there was still no answer. He sent up a prayer to the Lord. He was learning that that was the best way to handle these things. He would try again tomorrow.

Chapter Seven

When Debbie got to the hospital she was feeling much stronger in her faith. At least she thought she was . . . . until she looked at her precious daughter. Melisa was still lying there not moving, while the machines did their jobs. Debbie burst into tears and began sobbing out of control.

When Lil heard her, she came rushing in to see what was wrong. Lil could see that nothing had changed with Melisa. So she took Debbie in her arms and just held her. Lil soothed her with words of encouragement.

After a while Debbie tried to explain what had happened, "I don't know what's wrong with me. I felt so strong and up beat this morning and I was singing and praising with that CD you gave us. David and I said a real good prayer for Missy and then I came in here and . . . ." Debbie broke down again. "What kind of Christian am I? What kind of faith is that? As soon as I saw my daughter I just lost it."

Lil gently led Debbie out in the hall and held her some more. About that time Gladys came up. Lil explained to Gladys how Debbie and David had just accepted the Lord the night before.

Then Debbie started in again, "I'm so ashamed of myself, I know that I'm a child of God now. I felt so full of faith just this morning when I prayed for Missy. What's the matter with me?"

"Well for goodness sakes child you're just a baby Christian. You've got a lot of growin' to do. And anyway, that's just the devil tryin' to steal your joy." Gladys went on, "I'm just so proud of you. Now don't you be frettin' about your faith, you're doin' just fine."

Lil couldn't help but smile at Gladys's homey advice. She turned to Debra and suggested that they go into the chapel for a while. Debbie nodded and followed Lil to the hospital chapel.

It was a simple room with a small altar that had a cross behind it. And there were a few benches to sit on. After Debbie settled down, Lil turned to her and said, "Why don't you tell me about Melisa? What is she like?"

Lil could see the light come on in Debbie's eyes, as her thoughts went immediately to her little girl. "Oh," said Debbie, "She is so very special. The first thing people notice is that she is such a beautiful little girl. She has dark hair like her father and her eyes are a deep blue, but they seem to change with whatever color she wears. But once people get to know her and they look deeper, they become aware of how lovely she is on the inside. Missy is very sensitive and she has such a caring heart. She is very loving and . . . ." Debbie began to cry again, "Oh Lil, I love her so much."

"Of course you do. Thank you, for telling me about her. It will help us when we pray for her, to feel like we know her." Lil paused and then went on. "Debbie, I believe that God will bring her back to you. And now, would you like to hear a little about Amy?"

"Yes, please do tell me about her."

"I think the first thing everyone notices about Amy is she's always smiling, she has a very happy disposition. She absolutely embraces life and it's so easy for her to make friends. You already know her coloring is like mine, she's a strawberry blond with big brown eyes like her father's and I think she will be tall like me. It was always fun to take her picture because she likes to ham it up and yet she could be real serious when she would put on her best dress and become the perfect little model. Amy also, is very caring and always wants to help others." Lil stopped in her narration and took Debs hand before she went on. "I can't help thinking what a wonder pair our daughters are going to make."

After a while Lil told Debbie that she was going to lay her hands on her and pray for God to fill her with His peace. Lil prayed, "Lord I ask that Debbie be filled with the peace of God, the peace which passes all understanding. Thank you Lord, Amen."

Debra actually felt a peace come over her. She had just thanked Lil, when there was a tap on the door and Gladys burst into the room. "She's awake. Oh Debbie, little Missy's wakin' up. Come quickly she's askin' for her Mama!" . . . .

"Oh," Debbie cried, "My baby, Oh God my baby is awake. Thank you God, oh thank you." They all went running down the hall to Melisa's room. A doctor and a nurse were checking her blood pressure and her vital statistics.

As Debbie entered the room, the doctor looked up and said, "Everything looks good, her reflexes are good. Of course we will be running some test, so we will know more once we've done them. But it looks good Mrs. Miller."

Debbie barely heard what the doctor said. She was looking past him to Missy and then Missy saw her mother. "Mama," she cried out, "Mama."

Debra rushed forward to take her daughter into her arms. The tears came pouring out, but they were tears of joy. "Missy, oh sweetheart how do you feel? Are you in any pain? Oh my precious little girl, I love you so much."

Missy responded with, "Oh Mama, I love you too. And Mama," she said in a whisper, "I have something to tell you, something beautiful."

Just then, David burst into the room and joined his wife and daughter. He had been notified by the hospital as soon as Melisa had begun to wake up.

Out in the hall there were hugs all around. As Lil, Gladys and some of the other nurses joined in to celebrate the good news. "Missy was awake!" . . . .

Lil went into Amy's room and sat down on her bed, and with her fingers she brushed the hair back from her daughter's forehead. "Amy sweetheart, I'm sure you already know that Melisa is back here with her mother. I hope you won't miss her too much." Before Lil even knew it the tears let loose. Lil just couldn't help it. They were tears of joy and sadness.

"I'm sorry Lord. You know that I'm happy for the Millers. But oh God, I may need some extra encouragement right now. Thank you so much for sending Missy back to Debbie. She's only a baby Christian and this will surely strengthen hers and David's faith. Please give me strength. Lord you know I'm not jealous, but this is hard, oh so hard."

The next thing she knew, strong arms were pulling her up from the bed and holding her close. Gladys had come in, knowing that it would be hard for Lil, even though she would be overjoyed for the Millers.

"It's alright child. You just let those tears flow, they'll be helpin' you. The good Lord knows what you're goin' through and he also knows that you won't give up on your Amy and neither will I. We're just goin' a keep on sendin' up those prayers until we have her back with her mommy and daddy where she belongs."

Lil dried her tears and nodded in agreement to what Gladys had said. "Thank you Gladys. You know I am filled with joy for the Millers. It's just such an emotional thing. We had just finished praying when you came in to tell us that Melisa was waking up. Gladys, I'm so sorry to fall apart like this."

Gladys shook her head and said, "You've got nothin' to be sorry for. This was bound to shake you a little. You've been there for Debbie, David and for me and even for your hubby. Now it's my turn to hold you up a bit. So don't you go robbin' me of my chance to be (your support) for a change."

Then Gladys added, "Honey, I hope you don't mind but I took the liberty of callin' Peter. And he's on his way over, to take you out to lunch so you can have a little time to get yourself together. It'll be hard on the both of you, but I know you'll be just fine."

Peter came in shortly after that and took Lil to the park where they could be alone with their thoughts and spend some time just walking together.

Peter felt about the same as Lil. He was very happy for the Millers and he knew this would certainly strengthen their faith. It would also strengthen his and Lil's faith. However, they were still human. They didn't feel jealousy or envy. They just didn't want to hold back one little bit of joy for the Millers.

So they did what they always did when their own strength ran out. They went to their Savior and leaned on Him. As they remembered the scripture in *Matt. 11:28, (Come' to Me, all who are weary and are heavy—laden, and I will give you rest.)* and *Phil. 4:13, (I can do all thing through Him who strengthens me.)*

After Lil and Peter had spent some time just walking around the park, they began to get their perspective back. They had sought the Lord for strength, and then they both thanked Him for bringing Missy back to the Millers.

Once Lil had pulled herself together with the Lord's help, she came back to the hospital. Back to her daughter and back to the world's reality. Amy was still asleep. Even so, Lil held on to what she knew to be the truth. Having Missy wake up didn't change what they believed. They still had their faith, and they still had the God of miracles. They also still had an army of people praying for their little girl. And the fact that Missy had come back just proved even more than ever that; *(With God all things are possible).*

So now, Lil not only had her joy back, but she was more determined than ever to keep right on believing for Amy's full recovery. With that thought, Lil kissed her daughter and headed for Missy's room to share in their blessing.

Things had calmed down quite a bit in Missy's room and Lil found Debbie sitting quietly next to her daughter, who was now taking a nap. Debbie looked up as Lil entered the room. Then she said, "Lil, I wondered when you would come. Poor David had to go back to the school for a while to finish up some tests they were in the middle of."

Lil said, "That must have been very hard for him to leave Missy so soon."

"It was hard, but he will be back as soon as possible. You know I was almost afraid to let Missy go to sleep, but you can see her sleep is so different. Missy told me she had something she wanted to tell me, but I think the doctors tired her out with all the tests."

Lil sat down next to her new friend and said, "Peter came to take me to lunch and we went to the park. I figured you and David needed some time with Missy. I am truly happy for you. And I would have to say that you definitely got one of those blessings."

Debbie nodded but kept her eyes on her daughter. Almost as if she was afraid she would slip away again. Finally Debbie said, "Everything looks good so far, she has responded really well to all the tests. We may be able to take her home in a couple of days, and I can hardly wait."

Lil gave Debbie a hug and said, "This has turned out to be such a remarkable day. The entire hospital is buzzing with the excitement. You do know Debbie that this gives Peter and I hope too."

"Yes I suppose it does. I can't thank you enough for the support you've given us. You and Peter are the best friends we've ever had."

Lil patted Debbie's hand and went back to Amy's room. She wanted to talk to Amy about what had happened here today, even though she was pretty sure Amy already knew.

When Missy woke up from her nap she just beamed when she saw her mama sitting there with her favorite stuffed bunny. Missy reached out and took the bunny and buried her face in the soft pile.

Then she looked right at Debbie and crooked her finger, indicating she wanted her to lean closer. "Mama I want to tell you about something beautiful." she said this in a whisper, "I was in a garden and it was so beautiful, and there were real live bunnies. And Mama, there were lots of boys and girls there too and . . . ."

Missy hesitated as if she wasn't sure she should tell more. Debbie encouraged her to keep going. Then Missy said, "Mama for a little while, I was just a little bit afraid, only this much." She held up her thumb and finger about a half inch apart to show the smallness of her fear. "But Mama, there was this real nice man in the garden and he took my hand and he showed me all the animals. He showed me the flowers too. And then he took my fear away, cause he said that fear cannot stay in the garden."

As the tears began to flow Debbie said, "Oh my goodness honey. Did he tell you his name?"

Missy was watching her Mother as if she couldn't understand why she was crying. Then she got real close to Debbie and whispered in her ear, "He told me his name is Jesus."

Debbie, with tears still flowing, began to call out to the Lord, "Oh Jesus, thank you so much. Thank you for taking care of Missy and for sending her back to us."

Melisa didn't understand what was happening. She just sat there puzzling over her mother's reaction to her story. "Mama what's the matter? Do you know Jesus too? And why are you crying?"

Debra took Missy into her arms and tried to explain her emotions to her. "Yes honey, I do know Jesus and I'm crying because I'm so happy. You see, your papa and I have only recently gotten to know Jesus."

Missy asked, "Did you meet him in his garden? Cause I didn't know you were there."

Debbie shook her head. Not quite sure how to explain to Missy how she had met Jesus. "No sweetheart, your papa and I met Jesus while we were praying for you. This real nice lady told us that if we would ask Jesus to come into our hearts, then he would come in and always be with us."

Missy got very quiet again and then she said, "Did you Mama? Did you ask him to come in?"

"Yes darling we did. We asked him to come in to our hearts and be with us forever."

"Oh Mama I'm so glad. Maybe Jesus will come into my heart too, cause I don't know where his garden is. And I want him to be with me forever too!"

Out of the mouth of babes, thought Debbie. Then she said, "I'm sure he will." Then she looked up to see that David had been standing there listening.

"Do we have an incredible little girl or what?" he said. "I seem to have a knack at coming in when you are having these amazing spiritual talks with people."

"Papa," cried Missy, "Do you know Jesus too?"

"Absolutely I do know him and I met him the same way that your mama did. Now how is my little girl doing?"

Missy was not to be distracted. She looked intently at her parents and told them, "I want to ask Jesus into my heart. Can I Papa?"

Debbie looked at David and said, "I don't see why not." So right there in her hospital bed Melisa asked Jesus to come into her heart, so he would be with her forever. The little family spent the rest of the afternoon being thankful just to be together.

Chapter Eight

That evening Lil and Peter shared their feelings about this incredible day. They talked about how quickly things had changed for their new friends.

They notified the church about the good news. They wanted the people who had been praying for the Millers to share in their happiness.

Then Peter said, "You do still believe that everything will be alright with Amy, don't you? And Lil, I think it's alright to ask God why. We already talk to Him about everything anyway. And besides He already knows what we're thinking. So why not ask Him to help us understand. Why can't we have Amy home?"

"Of course you are right Peter. God knows we are but flesh and I admit that I had a hard time at first. I guess I wanted to ask God, why not Amy too? I still believe she's coming home. I just really want it to be soon. I miss her smiling face at the table every morning. And I want that back."

"I know. I feel the same way. Amy always had some funny little story that made me laugh. And when she felt I wasn't cooperating with something she wanted done she would put her hands on her hips and give me this look. Then she would tap her foot. Hum, I wonder where she got that from."

"Surely you're not suggesting that I . . . . ever used that look on you."

That lightened the mood a little and they headed up to bed.

As they lay in bed Peter's mind kept going back to the fun times they had with Amy. He turned toward Lil to see if she was still awake and saw that she lay there looking up at the ceiling. "Are you having trouble getting to sleep too?" he asked. "Now that we've gotten started, I just keep remembering some of cute things Amy would do and say."

Lil answered, "Yes, I know what you mean. She had such a great sense of humor for her age and she was so quick."

Peter nodded and then went on, "Remember when she was after me to build the tree house big enough for all her friends? So it could become their club house."

"Yes," Lil said, "I remember she was so fussy about everything. When I told her I would make her some curtains for the tree house she gave me that look you were talking about and said, 'Mommy, club houses don't have curtains.' She was very indignant that I would even suggest such a thing."

Peter had sat up and put the pillow behind him so he could lean against the headboard. "That's right. I remember she told me that you were trying to turn her club house into a play house for girls . . . . I had to laugh at that one, but then she caught me on the next one. She kept asking me if I was making it strong enough. I told her I was sure it would be plenty strong for all her little friends. Then she said, 'But what about you and Mommy? Will it be strong enough to hold you guys, because you're both pretty heavy?' That one caught me off guard."

Then Lil said, "She could be such a tomboy up until Sunday. Then she would put on one of her pretty dresses and turn into a little princess." After doing a lot of reminiscing about Amy they both concluded that they had a remarkable daughter.

They couldn't thank the Lord enough for giving her to them. And they believed that He would give her back to them because they were standing on His promises.

They went to the gospel of *Mark 11:24, (Therefore I say to you, what things for which you pray and ask, believe that you have received them, and they shall be granted you.)* So they prayed one more time.

Also going to the scripture in *Phil. 4:6, 7 (Be anxious for nothing, but in everything by prayer and supplication with thanksgiving, let your request be made known to God, And the peace of God, which surpasses all comprehension, shall guard your hearts and your minds in Christ Jesus.)*

After putting Amy in God's capable hands Lil and Peter were finally able to fall asleep with the Lord's peace in their hearts.

I was aware that I was sleeping, but I kept smelling roses. The scent was so strong and then I felt the touch of a rose by my cheek. I opened my eyes expecting to see Peter with a rose in his hand. I said, "Peter what are you . . . ."

Then I realized that it wasn't Peter at all, it was Amy. Amy giggled and said, "It's me, Mommy. Why did you think it was Daddy?"

"I guess because your father used to bring me roses all the time when we first got married and he would sometimes wake me up like you just did with just one rose."

Amy cocked her head to one side thoughtfully and said, "Oh Mommy that is so romantic. Daddy must love you a whole bunch. Then Amy asked, "Did you know that the roses here don't have any thorns?"

I responded with, "I suppose it would be that way, here in the Garden of Blessings . . . . Honey, do you realize that Melisa came back to her mommy and daddy yesterday?"

Amy was quiet for a moment before she said, "Yes I know, because we all met in the field of blessings to say goodbye to her." And then Amy turned away from her mother before she said, "Mommy I do like it here, but I miss you and Daddy so much."

I was up in a flash from the bench I had been resting on. I reached out for Amy but there was nothing there. "Amy where are you? Amy?"

"Wake up Lil, you're okay. You must have been dreaming again." Lil threw herself into her husband's arms and said, "Peter, oh Peter, she told me that she wants to come home."

Peter said, "She said that? She told you that she wants to come home? Oh Lil, surely the Lord will help her come home then."

Lil got up and started pacing the floor. Then she stopped and looked at Peter before saying, "Well to be honest she didn't exactly say she wanted to come home. She told me, 'that she likes it there, but that she misses us,' and then I reached out for her and she was gone. What does it mean Peter? I don't know what to do next."

They both held on to each other for a long time, and then Peter finally said, "We do what we've always done. We keep on holding on to God."

Lil and Peter got up early that morning. Then after they had their breakfast they headed over to the hospital together. When they got out of the car and headed inside, Peter put his arm around Lil and asked, "Are you going to be alright?"

Lil nodded and answered, "Yes, I will be fine." Since they were early, there were not many people about yet. As they entered their daughter's room they were surprised to see one perfectly shaped rose laying on Amy's bed.

"Oh my," gasped Lil. She began to look about for more roses but she found none. There was only the one perfect rose.

"Do you think it's a sign?" Peter asked, "Or maybe Gladys put it there."

"I don't know Peter. I don't know what to think about the things that have happened in the last couple of days. I wish I knew what it all means. I will ask Gladys if she or one of the other nurses might have put it there."

Peter stepped closer to the bed and touched the rose as if he thought it might just disappear. But it was real, so he gently picked it up and handed it to Lil. She took it from him and carefully examined it then she looked up and said softly, "It doesn't have any thorns. Amy told me that the roses in the heavenly garden don't have any thorns."

Gladys chose that minute to walk into the room. She stopped short, surprised to see Amy's parents there so early. "Well good mornin'," she said as she went over to check Amy's monitor, "It's mighty early for you folks to be here, especially on a Saturday."

Both Lil and Peter just stood there. They were still a little stunned by the perfect rose with no thorns. Peter responded, "Sorry Gladys. Good morning to you too and you're right, it is a little earlier than we normally get here."

Then Lil asked, "Uh Gladys, did you by any chance leave this rose on Amy's bed?"

Gladys frowned and then inspected the rose before saying, "Nope it wasn't me. You say you found it on her bed? That is strange. Because I was just in here a minute ago and it wasn't there then. Now where do you suppose it came from? Aw, I'll bet your just funnin' me and you brought that rose in here yourselves. Now didn't you?"

"No Gladys, we didn't." responded Peter. "We have no idea where it came from. Perhaps one of the other nurses brought it in?"

Gladys was shaking her head, "Nope, I'm sure I would have seen them."

Lil gave up trying to figure it out for the time being. She sat down next to Amy and took her hand. Then she began to talk to her like she always did. Peter sat down on the other side of the bed and spoke lovingly to his little girl.

After Peter had gotten a ride home with a friend, Debbie poked her head in the door and asked if it was alright to come in. "Of course it's alright. How are things going with Melisa?"

"Actually," Deb said, "That's one of the reason I'm here. Missy wants to meet the lady that told her mama about Jesus."

Lil responded with surprise, "Are you serious?"

Then Debbie went on to tell Lil that when Melisa woke up, she told them about meeting Jesus in his garden. And she was so happy that her mama and daddy knew him too, because they had received him into their hearts. "And now she wants to meet you."

53

Lil stood up and followed Debbie. She could actually feel the joy that she saw on Debbie's face. "I'm sure both of you must be overcome with excitement."

As she entered Missy's room she saw one of the prettiest little girls she had ever seen. Missy was sitting up and her dark brown hair hung in soft curls around her face. Missy looked up at Lil and her face shown like an angel.

Missy seemed a little shy. Then she said softly, "Hello Mrs. Iverson. How are you today?"

So very polite and sweet thought Lil. Lil moved closer to the bed and then she responded, "I'm just fine, thank you. Your mother told me that you got to see Jesus."

Melisa nodded and then she said, "Yes, I got to meet him in his garden. He was so nice to me and he took my fear away. I uh, wanted to thank you for telling Mama about Jesus. Did you know that I asked Jesus to come into my heart too?"

Lil almost lost it when Missy said that. But she blinked away the tears and answered, "Oh Missy that is so wonderful. When did that happen?"

"Last night when Papa came in and told me that he knew Jesus too. And then he told me that Jesus would be with them forever. So I wanted Jesus to be with me forever too."

Lil was very happy for this lovely family. After a while she got up to leave and Debbie went with her into the hall and said, "I hope it helped you to hear Missy talk about the garden. It sure sounds a lot like the garden in your dreams, and then when she said that Jesus took away her fear. Isn't that, what Amy told you?"

"Yes it is exactly what Amy told me when she talked about Melisa. And you're right, it does help. Although I've always believed what I was seeing in the garden was a reality and I felt it was more than just a dream. But it does help to have it confirmed by one of God's little ones. Thanks Debbie, you have a beautiful little girl."

"Thank you Lil, I am so happy right now I feel like I'm floating." . . . .

Lil phoned Peter at home. She told him about Melisa and how she had asked Jesus into her heart. "Isn't that just about the sweetest thing you ever heard? I still remember when Amy got us out of bed that one Sunday night. She said she didn't want to go to sleep until she knew she was saved."

Peter chuckled and said, "Yes, I do remember how serious Amy was." Then he asked Lil, "Anything else on the rose? Did you ask Debbie about it?"

Lil said, "Yes, I asked Debbie if she knew where it came from. She said she had no idea." Then Lil told Peter something that she discovered about the rose. "It has thorns Peter, but they just didn't get hard the way thorns usually do on a mature stem. I've never seen anything like it. So I have chosen to believe that either Amy or an angel left it on Amy's bed."

Peter said, "I can agree with that. The last few days have been so incredible. I say we keep on believing for one more miracle. What do you think?"

On the other end of the phone Lil said, "I say Amen, to one more miracle." . . . .

Lil stopped in before she headed home to say goodbye to Debbie. "Hey," she said as she tapped at Melisa's door, "I thought I'd stop and say good night." Lil saw that Missy was asleep so she quietly came into the room.

Debbie gave her a big smile and motioned her to come and sit down for a minute. Then she told Lil, "The doctor said we can take her home tomorrow."

"That's great. I'm really happy for you. She is a lovely little girl and bright as a button. I'm sure you must be very proud of her."

Debbie sat looking at Missy as if she couldn't quite believe her own good fortune. She nodded and said, "I don't have the words to tell you how very blessed we feel right now. It was just a little over a week ago that things looked so grim. And I can't begin to thank you and Peter enough for what you've helped us find. I know of course that you will tell me to give God the glory and believe me I do. But without your support, this past week would have been unbearable."

Lil sat there quietly, and then finally said, "Remember what you said the other day about not believing in coincidences? Well, I have pretty much come to the conclusion that the Lord orchestrated our meeting like this, in order to bless both families. Deb, you must be aware of how it has blessed both Peter and me to see you and David come to the Lord. And then we got blessed again when He brought Missy back. Other than Amy, I would have to say that helping others find the Lord has become our main focus. So we need to thank you and David as well."

Debra rose and put her arms around Lil and then just held on for quite a while. When she let go she said to Lil, "You are such a gracious lady. I hope we will continue to be the best of friends."

Lil answered, "I'm sure we will be." Then she said good night and went home to Peter. But right before she left, she went back to Amy's room one more time to put the perfect rose back on her daughter's bed.

By the time she got home she had gone over everything she could remember about these last few days. "Yes," she said to herself, "This has been the Lord's work, all the way. Thank you, Father. You do work in mysterious ways."

The following morning the hospital was all a buzz because Melisa was going home. All the papers had been signed and one by one the nurses had come in to say their private goodbyes to one of their little angels.

Last but definitely not least Gladys came in with a package all wrapped up in pretty pink paper for Missy. She had tears in her eyes when she handed her gift to Missy. Gladys said, "I'm sure goin' a miss your sweet face. You are an inspiration to the rest of us to smile more."

Melisa looked puzzled then said, "What's a spearation?"

Everyone laughed as her mother tried to explain the new word to her daughter. Missy wasn't all that worried about the meaning anyway, she was too busy pulling the paper from her gift. She opened the box carefully and gasped when she saw a pretty little angel music box. She said, "Oh Gladys It is so beautiful. Can I please play it?"

Gladys said, "Of course you can. And it plays, (Yes Jesus loves me.)"

Missy cried, "Oh I love that song!" Debbie and David looked at each other and shook their heads. But Missy cleared it up by saying, "We sang that in the garden all the time." Then they all heard the familiar melody playing.

In a few minutes David wheeled Missy out into the hall. Debbie slipped away from the excitement and went over to Lil to say goodbye. Lil looked up, her eyes brimming with tears.

"Oh Lil I'm so sorry. I have been so wrapped up in my own happiness. I wasn't thinking how hard this must be for you."

Lil spoke up, "No it isn't that. I am just so overcome with joy for you and besides we get to take Amy home tomorrow. And Debbie, I'm more convinced than ever that God orchestrated our meeting like this."

Just then David came up with Missy in her wheelchair, and said, "Are we ready?"

Missy said a polite goodbye to Lil and then they headed for the door. But Missy suddenly cried out, "No, Papa wait," then she motioned for Debbie to lean close and said, "I want to see Amy before I go."

There were stunned looks all around, because no one had mentioned Amy to Missy. They were worried that it might upset her. She had not known that Lil had a daughter. Missy tried to get up but her father stopped her. "Mama she's here somewhere. I know she is, cause she told me so. Please, I want to see her."

Finally they all agreed that she needed to see Amy. They explained to her that Amy wouldn't be able to respond to her. But Missy simply said, "She will know I'm there."

They took Missy into Amy's room. Since the wheelchair was too low for her to see Amy, David lifted her out of the chair and onto Amy's bed. She reached out her little hand and patted Amy on her shoulder. Then she told Amy about her mama and papa getting saved and meeting Jesus.

Missy hesitated for a minute and then she asked Lil, "Are you Amy's mama?" Lil nodded and then Missy asked her, "Would it be okay if I play the music box for Amy?"

Lil said, "Yes honey that would be nice. I'm sure she will like that."

And so Missy played the little angel music box for Amy and then she leaned over and kissed Amy on her cheek. David lifted her back into the wheelchair as she called out one last word for Amy. "I love you Amy. I will pray for you every day."

Chapter Nine

Monday morning both Lil and Peter went into the hospital to talk to Amy's doctor because it was time to transfer her back home again. As they sat in Dr. Gordman's office waiting for him to come in, they were a bit nervous. They knew he would use all the medical terms they had become so very familiar with. However, they had information that he simply did not possess. They had a higher power and authority that had told them to never give up on their daughter.

That's why they continued to care for her at home even though the doctor would recommend a nursing home. They looked up as he entered his office. He shook hands with both of them and then he sat down behind his desk and opened Amy's file.

He studied it for a minute then look up at the Iversons and said, "I'm sure your anxious to get this over with so that you can take Amy home and get her settled." They both nodded. Then he went on, "We have already discussed putting Amy into some sort of care facility and since I already know how you feel about that, I'll just move on to what we have found in this last visit."

Again the Iversons nodded but they said nothing. So Dr. Gordman continued, "You know that Amy has always been a puzzle to me and the rest of the staff, because we've never really had another patient like her. She simply doesn't fit in any of the medical books on comas."

Lil and Peter did know this and they also knew the reason for her unusual condition. She was much more stable than most patients who had been comatose for as long as Amy had. The reason was totally spiritual. They also knew it was very difficult for a person trained in medicine to understand this. Doctor Gordman had been through all of this with them before and he knew there was no shaking the Iverson's stand on how to care for their daughter.

So he simply stated, "We found nothing during her stay here that would alarm us. There were no infections, nothing unusual. However, I do need to tell you that yesterday morning there was a slight variation in her brain function. This sometimes happens but what it means we aren't sure. It could mean nothing, but I felt I should mention it. Having shared that, I can see no reason why you can't have her back home. If that's what you want."

Peter and Lil both responded, "Yes, absolutely."

Dr. Gordman stood and shook their hands again. He told them he would arrange for Amy to be moved. Then he paused at the door and said, "I must say I admire you both. You are a remarkable couple and Amy is fortunate to have you as her parents. I sincerely hope that your prayers are being heard." And with that he was gone.

Lil and Peter had both picked up on the mention of the change in Amy's brain function. Even though the doctor had said it could mean nothing, they knew it could also mean a great deal.

They followed Doctor Gordman out into the hall to wait for the transfer to be arranged. They would follow the emergency vehicle home and wait for the technicians to do their job. And then they would begin the spiritual battle for Amy's recovery once again. This was a battle that had begun almost twenty two months ago . . . .

By the second month of Amy's coma the doctors had pretty much given up any hope that Amy would ever wake up. They had said that even if she did wake up, her body would never function properly. Simply stated, there wasn't much hope. That however was in the natural. And that was when the Lord had spoken to Lil, and said, *"Don't ever give up on Amy."* So Amy's mother and father had told the enemy that they were not giving up. In fact they would never give up because they knew, *(With God all things are Possible.)* And so with the support of their church, their family and friends, the Iversons had set out on the spiritual battle of their lives.

Monday morning at the Millers was a very happy morning indeed. Missy was a little weak, so she had her cereal in bed surrounded by her many stuffed animals. Debbie couldn't take her eyes off of her daughter.

After a while David said, "You know Deb, eventually you're going to have to go on with your life. You can't follow Missy around forever."

Debbie said, "I know . . . . but not just yet. We just got her back yesterday. You can't blame me for doing a little hovering."

David leaned over and kissed Melisa and then his wife before saying, "I guess you're right. I know I'll be glad when I'm able to relax enough to sleep through the night. I must have gotten up five or six times last night to check on her." Then David asked, "Have we thanked God this morning for bringing her back?"

"Only about a hundred times but I still don't think that's enough." And then Debbie added, "David, I can't help but wonder how Lil and Peter are doing. They were supposed to get Amy back home today. I sure wish she would wake up too. I just don't know how they do it."

David glanced at Missy and then motioned Deb out in the hall before saying, "I know what you mean. I know they have tremendous faith but to keep on going day after day for almost two years. I sure don't want to lose touch with them. I want us to continue our Bible study even if we don't stay at their church. I just hope it won't be too hard for them to keep seeing us."

Debbie went into the kitchen giving what David said some serious thought before she answered, "I don't believe that Lil would allow our blessing to stop her from ministering to us. She is just too strong in her faith to let anything stand in her way and I think Peter is the same way."

David poured them some coffee and then sat down at the kitchen table before saying, "Of course you're right. I can't get over how they were there for us, at just the right time."

Debbie said, "I guess I haven't told you what Lil thinks about all of this. She is absolutely sure that God orchestrated our meeting up with them. She also said that now there would be two more Christians praying for Amy."

"No Mama. Now there will be three more Christians praying for Amy." Both of Missy's parents were on their feet in seconds surprised by Missy's declaration.

"Yes Missy, you are right. Now there are three new Christians praying for your little friend. But what are you doing out of bed? You know you have to stay quiet a few more days. And then next week you get to start first grade."

Missy looked sad and then she said, "I don't understand why Amy is still sick. She told me before I left the garden that she was in the same hospital as me. She said she was still sleeping, but that I shouldn't worry . . . . cause," Missy paused a minute then she shrugged her shoulders before she went on more softly, "Cause Amy said someday we're going to be best friends."

The Millers just stood there not knowing what to say. They had already come to the conclusion that nothing was out of the realm of possibilities. Finally Debbie asked, "So you didn't hear the nurses talking about a little girl named Amy?"

Missy shook her head. "No Mama, I even asked them if there were any other little girls in the hospital. But they said I shouldn't worry about any of that. That's why when we were leaving I remembered and I knew that she was there. So I wanted to say goodbye to her, cause someday she's going to be my best friend."

At about three o'clock Monday afternoon Debbie's cell phone rang. She picked it up and said, "Hello this is Debra."

It was Gladys on the line. "Hi, I hope I'm not interruptin' anythin'. I know I shouldn't be callin' and I'm probably breakin' some sort of rule. But I decided to take a chance since you did give me your cell phone number so I could always locate you. Anyway, I just had to find out how that little angel is doin'. I became so attached to her while she was here."

Debra was pleased to hear from Gladys or Granny as some of the nurses had started calling her because she just loved those little ones so much. "Don't you worry about that Gladys, I'm very glad to hear from you. And Missy is doing great. She has been telling her stuffed animals and her dolls all about her trip to (the garden).

"What do you think she saw Gladys? Do you think she was dreaming? But if that's the case then how did she know about Amy? She told us that no one told her that Amy was in the hospital and she even asked some of the nurses. They had told her she shouldn't worry. I know Lil didn't mentioned Amy to Missy either. So she must have talked to Amy in the garden. I guess it is just another miracle."

Gladys nodded enthusiastically, even though she was talking to Debbie on the phone. "That's exactly what it is. It's a miracle. I have always thought that these little ones are so close to God that it's nothin' for them to spend time with Him in heaven. And anyway it says in the Bible that the apostle Paul talked about himself bein' caught up into heaven. It says he doesn't know if he was in his body or not, but he does know he was caught up into paradise. Now that sounds a lot like Missy's garden to me. So I agree with Lil when she says, 'If it's based on the Bible, then there's a possibility it can still happen today'."

Debbie said, "Gladys, this is so neat, between you and Lil I keep learning new things everyday,"

Then Gladys asked, "Speakin' of Lil have you talked to her since you left the hospital?"

"No," Debbie replied, "I know I need to call her but it's just so awkward, because Amy's home coming couldn't have been as joyful as our bringing Missy home."

Gladys said, "Well I have just the thing to make it easier. You can tell Lil what happened on Sunday mornin' when Missy went to say goodbye to Amy. In fact I'm pretty sure it was when Missy played her music box for Amy."

Debbie prompted Gladys, "What? Tell me what happened?"

"Well, it was right after you all left. I noticed a slight change on Amy's brain monitor. Now I'm no expert at readin' brain scans, but I think Amy was reactin' to Missy."

"Oh Gladys, that is good news. Isn't it? Surely it must mean something if she was able to react. Maybe she's trying to come back. We need to pray for God to help Amy."

Debbie should be used to her daughter's sudden appearances. But she was always startled by her little voice that seemed to come out of nowhere. "Mama, what does Amy need help with?" Missy wanted to know.

"Honey, I'll tell you about that in a minute. Right now there is someone on the phone that would love to say hello to you."

"Who is it Mama? Who is it?" Debbie handed the phone to Missy and watched as she said a timid hello. Then Missy cried out, "Gladys, I love the music box so much. And guess what? I get to start the first grade pretty soon."

As Missy talked to Gladys, Debbie wondered how she would tell Lil what she had just found out. She asked for the Lord's help.

Chapter Ten

Lil sat at the desk in her small office off the family room. She was trying to catch up on some paper work from her dress shop. Lil thought back to the day she had opened her shop. The clothes she designed were up scale and somewhat pricey. She had been designing clothes ever since she was in high school. Lil is tall and slim and could just as easily have been a model, but she preferred designing for others.

Then she had gone on to a small Art School that specialized in design arts and computer graphics. They had recommended that she go into magazine design.

Her focus however had remained on fashion. She enjoyed first creating the design on paper and then watching it come to life on her sewing machine. At first she had done it just for herself and a few friends. It didn't take long before she was getting requests to please do a special dress for someone's daughter, or granddaughter.

It finally got to where she simply couldn't keep up. That's when she hired a couple of girls to do the sewing, so she could concentrate solely on designing. Then the business just grew from there. Her dress shop, simply named (Lil's Fashions), took off until she finally had to hire even more help.

She credited her success to the Lord. He had given her the talent. The shop was still doing well but her heart just hadn't been in it ever since Amy had her accident. "Lord, I would give it up in a minute, just to have her back."

Just then the phone rang and Lil picked it up on the first ring. "Hello." She was pleased to hear Debbie on the line. She turned away from her work and asked Debbie, "How is Missy doing?"

Debbie answered with a smile in her voice, "She is just so busy getting reacquainted with all her dolls and stuffed animals. I have heard the story of the garden told from every perspective . . . . But Lil, I want to know how you're feeling? You have come to mean so much to me."

"Hey, I'm doing fine. It makes it so much easier having Amy at home. And right now I'm busy catching up on paper work from the dress shop."

Debra said, "I would sure love to see your shop some time. If you let me know when you're going to be there, I might even buy something special for our anniversary next month."

Lil pulled a sketch from her desk and said, "I have just the dress for you. I will give it to the seamstress right away and she can have it ready for you to see in a few of days."

Debra was in awe, "Wow, I've never had a dress designed especially for me. I can hardly wait."

Lil responded with, "You haven't even seen it yet."

"Lil I trust your sense of style completely . . . . But listen Lil, there is something that I would like to tell you. I just got off the phone with Gladys. She had called to see how Missy was doing and she told me something I think you should know." . . . .

"Oh really, that sounds kind of ominous . . . . Please tell me what she said."

Debbie quickly responded. "Oh, I don't think it's bad at all Lil. Gladys told me that right after we left with Melisa she was in Amy's room and she noticed there had been a small change on her brain monitor. She checked the time and she is certain it was exactly when Missy was playing the music box. So that means Amy was reacting. Doesn't it?"

Lil sat very still, remembering what Doctor Gordman had said, "It could mean nothing."

The silence had been long enough that Debbie said, "Lil, are you okay? Am I wrong? I thought it was a good thing."

"It is a good Debbie. I'm sure of it. Amy's doctor had told us about it but he had said it probably didn't mean anything. But he doesn't know what we do, about the garden and about the song the children sing. And Dr. Gordman doesn't know about the connection between two very special little girls. Yes Debbie, I think this is very good news."

The next morning Lil told Peter about her conversation with Debbie and what Gladys had said about the monitor. Peter was pleased to hear what Gladys had to say and his response was, "It sure sounds like Amy was reacting to that song. I've been trying to think if there is something we could do to touch that part of Amy."

Lil said, "Yes Peter I agree. But even more than the song, I think she was reacting to Missy. There is definitely a connection between the two of them. Remember Amy was aware of Missy the first night she was at the hospital."

"Yes that's right. Perhaps we should try and get the two of them together. Do you think it would be wrong to ask Debbie?"

"No Peter. I'm sure that Debbie would be happy to have Missy visit Amy. And since I am having a dress made up for Debbie I thought perhaps . . . ."

Peter looked up with surprise, "What? When did this happen? And why is it that you women are always way ahead of us guys?"

"Hum, I suppose it's because we are much more sensitive than you macho guys are." Lil grinned at her somewhat perplexed husband. Then she replied, "Yesterday when I talked to Debbie she mentioned she would like to come to the shop some time. And she told me that she and David are having an anniversary next month and she would like a new dress. And I just happened to have the perfect dress sketched out right in front of me. So I'm planning to call her and work out a way for Missy to come and spend some time with Amy. Then Debbie and I could go on over to the shop. Of course that would mean that you would have to watch the girls for a little while. Would that be okay with you?"

As usual Peter was just a bit stunned at the way Lil got things done. He simply said, "I would be happy to help out. And now I will leave it all in your capable hands. I think I had better get to work where I at least have a clue what I'm doing." With that he kissed Lil goodbye and headed out the door.

Lil was about to look up Debbie's number when the phone rang. She picked it up. "Hello." It was Debbie on the line. Lil said, "I was just looking for your number to call you. What's up?"

Debbie answered, "There are a couple of things on my mind. First I'm wondering how you would feel about my bringing Missy over to visit with Amy. Missy really wants to come and I thought it might help in reaching Amy. What do you think?"

Lil responded, "I think great minds think alike. That was a big part of why I was going to call you."

Debbie laughed, "Hey that makes me feel real good, to be on the same wave length as you."

Lil went on to say, "I also faxed the design I want for you to my best seamstress. I told her you look like a perfect size eight. Is that about right?" (Debbie was a petite five-five, and had hair the color of wheat.)

Deb said, "It sure is and I can hardly wait."

Then Lil said, "She was going to get right on it. So she should have it ready by tomorrow. Can you come over here tomorrow afternoon? Peter will be here to watch the girls. We could go over to my shop and you could try on the dress. Is that okay, with you?"

All Debbie could say was, "Lil, I guess you read my mind, because wanting to see your shop was the other thing I was going to ask you about. While I'm just thinking about it you've already got it all organized and yes that sounds great to me. Would it be alright if David comes along? He can give Peter a hand with the girls. How does that sound?"

The two women agreed that they had everything worked out and they would all meet up at the Iverson's home at four o'clock the next day. But it was Missy who was thrilled. She was going to see Amy.

It was just a few minutes before four when Peter saw the Millers head up the front walk with little Melisa leading the way. She was carrying some picture books under her arm and pulling

David along as fast as she could. Peter opened the door just before they got to the porch. He said, "Hello Missy. It looks like you're anxious to get here."

Missy stopped trying to drag her father up the stairs and answered, "Yes, Mr. Iverson. Sometimes my Papa is kind of slow and I can't wait to see Amy. Did you tell her that I was coming?"

That took everyone by surprise except for Lil. And she leaned down and took Missy's hand and said, "Yes, I told her that Melisa was coming over to spend some time with her and I'm sure that made her very happy. Do you want to stay out here with us for a while or do you want to go right to Amy's room?"

"Thank you Mrs. Iverson, but I really want to go see Amy." That declaration set off smiles all around. So without further ado, Lil lead Missy upstairs to Amy's room."

David handed his jacket to Peter who also took Debbie's wrap. Then David said, "She been like this all day. She couldn't wait to come over."

Then Debbie added, "It's as if she has a mission. I do think she believes that she can help Amy."

Lil walked back into the room just in time to hear the end of the conversation. She joined in, "You know Debbie, she just might be right. Peter and I talked a lot about what happened with the brain monitor and I definitely think that Amy was responding more to Missy than she was to the music box. Of course it could have been a combination, but in my dreams Amy talked about Melisa the very first night she was brought in. So there seems to be a strong connection. It's given us a glimmer of hope so we're hanging on. Now does anyone want some coffee or tea?"

They visited for a short time and then Lil and Debbie got their coats to head over to Lil's shop. They told Missy they were going, and she simply said "Bye Mama, I'll see you later." She was sitting on the bed with her back propped up with a pillow against the headboard and she was (reading) from a picture book that she had mostly memorized.

Debbie laughed, "She has started to learn to read a little but to listen to her you would think she could read the newspaper."

Lil drove them to her shop. She pulled into a parking place right out front so that Debbie could see both the sign and the windows.

"Oh Lil, the shop is lovely. I don't know what I expected but this is so elegant. I'm not sure I can afford one of your designs."

Lil smiled. She was proud of her little shop. They went in through the front door so Debbie could see it from a customer's view point. Debbie was like a kid in a candy store admiring all that she saw. There was more than just clothing. There were a lot of accessories, shoes, handbags, belts, and of course lots of jewelry. Debbie said, "Wow I hardly know what to say Lil, but you sure have great taste."

Lil said, "Excuse me a minute. I'll just go in the back and get the dress I have in mind for you." With that she disappeared behind a curtain, only to return with a lovely burgundy colored dress with a very simple line. Lil held it up to Debbie. Then she said, "I think the color is good with your blond hair. What do you think?"

Debbie took it from Lil and went over to a full length mirror to hold it up. It was very simple and yet so elegant. She turned to Lil and said, "What can I say? I've never had anything cut this beautifully before."

Lil turned Debbie toward the dressing rooms and said, "Well go try it on. Let's see how it fits." Debbie came out after a couple of minutes wearing the burgundy dress. It fell just a little below the knees. It had long fitted sleeves with a jewel neckline and it fit Debbie perfectly.

Lil had no trouble figuring out if Debbie liked the dress or not. Debbie's face was lit up with approval. So Lil said, "Do you want to look at some accessories while we're here? Everything is half price to friends."

Debbie felt like a princes. But she shook her head and said, "I think this is all the elegance I can handle for one day. Lil, I guess you know that I love this dress even if I have to pay for it in installments."

Lil laughed and said, "Not to worry. I give really good discounts to special people."

At the Iverson's home, Peter was having quite a discussion with David as they poured over the scriptures. It turned out that Debbie had shared with David the discussion that she had with Gladys. Where Gladys had talked about how Paul was caught up into the third heaven.

David might be a baby Christian but he could ask some really tough questions like, "What does it mean the third heaven? Does that mean there are three heavens?" David asked Peter.

"Whoa," Peter said, "You might be getting in a little deep for a new Christian. Why don't we just stick to the fact that Paul went to the third heaven, which he also called Paradise. And apparently he went there in the spirit. And I believe Paul told us about it so that we would know that it's a real place and that it is still possible to go there and visit. And I agree with Gladys, that more than likely the Garden of Blessings is in heaven."

David thought about what Peter said. Then he asked, "So then, do you think that Melisa's and Amy's spirits met in heaven?"

Peter considered the question carefully before he answered, "Yes I do. I don't pretend to understand how it all works, but I do believe they met in a heavenly garden. I also believe they are somehow still connected, because of what happened at the hospital when Amy responded to Missy."

David shook his head and said, "This is all so amazing. Just a couple of weeks ago, I wouldn't have believed any of this, but now I do believe it. And you're right, that Missy feels a strong connection to Amy. I agree with what Deb said, about Missy feeling like she on a mission. I think that's exactly how she feels. And she believes her mission is to help Amy come back to you and Lil. She is very adamant that we are to focus on praying Amy back home."

Peter said, "Well, don't ever underestimate the faith of a child. Children, by the simple act of childlike faith, have turned families around. I have seen it happen. Besides that's what faith is. It's a simple act of trust and who does that any better than a child?"

Just then the door opened and Lil and Debbie came in. Debbie was carrying a big box that said, Lil's Fashions on it. "What's this?" David asked, but he was all smiles to see Debbie so happy. There was a lot of excited talk as Debbie told David about Lil's beautiful shop.

Debbie was all excited when she said, "Oh David, you really need to see Lil's shop. It's absolutely stunning."

"Now why would I need to see a ladies dress shop?" David teased.

Debbie just grinned and said, "So you'll know where to shop for your wife of course." And then she showed off the dress that Lil had designed just for her.

When things settled down they decided to order pizza and just keep the evening going. Missy had a piece of pizza but insisted she had to stay in Amy's room and keep her company. In about an hour Missy came out of Amy's room and went over to Lil and said, "Amy wants Toby, but I don't know where he is."

Lil looked a little puzzled. But it was Debbie who spoke up and asked Missy, "Honey, did Amy speak to you? How did you know what she wanted?"

Missy put her head down the way she often did if she thought she had said something wrong. Then she looked up at Debbie and said, "I'm sorry Mama. I just know what she wants."

"Oh sweetheart it's okay you didn't do anything wrong. We just wondered how you knew." Debbie took Missy into her arms.

Then Lil rushed over to reassure Missy. "It's okay Missy, we just forget how well you understand Amy."

Then Missy said, "Amy doesn't talk to me, but she likes to hear me talk about the garden. Cause I still remember all about it."

Lil glanced at Debbie and then said to Missy, "Why don't we go and get Toby for Amy and then maybe you could tell your mommy and me about the garden. Would that be okay?" Missy nodded and took her mama's hand and led her to Amy's room.

Lil reached up on the shelf and got Toby down. Missy put Toby in the crook of Amy's little arm and then settled on the bed next to Amy again. "What would you like to hear about the garden?" She asked.

Lil looked over at Debbie and then said, "Whatever you would like to tell us would be fine."

Missy sat thinking for a minute then she brightened, and said, "It's really beautiful and it's filled with flowers and lots of real live animals." Then she added more softly, "And there are angels that sometimes come to the garden." Missy was almost whispering as she talked about the angels. She hesitated until Debbie encouraged her to go on.

Missy looked at Amy and then at Lil, before she leaned over to her mama and whispered, "They come to get the blessings." Then she clapped her hands over her mouth, as if she might have revealed a great secret.

Lil had tears flowing down her cheeks as she said, "Oh Missy, thank you sweetheart. That is truly a beautiful story. It's no wonder Amy likes to hear it so much."

After the Millers went home, Lil sat in Amy's room just touching her daughter and wondering what it all meant. "Oh Lord, I know that you are aware of what has happened here and you have sent this precious little girl to be Amy's friend. Thank you Lord, thank you for being there and for caring.

Lil just sat quietly for a few minutes before she said, "Lord is it wrong for me to want more? No, no, no Lord, because, you are still the God of miracles. And I couldn't have begun to hold on to your promise for all this time, without your being with me every step of the way. You put the promise into my heart Lord and I will never let it go. Our little girl is coming all the way back to us and we will never give up." . . . .

Meanwhile, when the Millers got home David carried a sleeping Missy into the house and into her bedroom. Debbie came in and settled her daughter into bed and kissed her cheek. Missy suddenly sat up with her eyes wide open and said, "No Mama, I haven't said my prayers yet and we all need to pray for Amy."

Debbie could only smile at her little girl, who seemed to already have a better handle on how to trust God than her mother did. David came back into the bedroom and they all got down on their knees by Missy's bed. And they sent some very heart felt prayers to their heavenly Father for a little girl that they wanted so much to be whole again . . . .

A very similar scene was taking place at the Iversons, as both Lil and Peter had suddenly felt a strong need to get down on their knees, before the Lord to hold Amy up in prayer. And so once again Lil and Peter stood on the promises of God for their daughter. And so it was that the two family's prayers were joined together and sent to heaven.

Chapter Eleven

◆

Lil had drifted off to sleep with thanksgivings still on her lips, as her thoughts went over what Missy had said about the garden and the angels that would come and get the blessings.

In just a little while I found myself in the garden. I was sitting on the bench and I was reading once again.

Toby, where are you hiding? I want you to come see this butterfly, it is so pretty." Toby knew he was well hidden behind the painted daisies, but he decided to come charging out just then to see if he could startle his mistress. But she just squealed and bent down and scooped him up in her arms to show him the bright blue butterfly that she had been admiring. He had to admit it was pretty, but then it seemed to Toby that everything in the garden was not just pretty, but exquisite.

Just then I heard the children and I looked up to see Amy coming towards me. Amy said, "Hi Mommy, I was hoping you would be here."

I stood up. I wanted more than anything to reach out and hold Amy but instead I asked her, "Could we just take a walk around the garden for a while? I never have been able to see much of it."

Amy nodded, and led the way down a path that had lilac bushes on both sides. Amy picked one and put it in her hair. I looked at the bush where Amy had picked the bloom and I was almost certain that it had grown right back. I just shook my head and kept following Amy. I finally asked Amy, "How are you honey? Do you miss being with Melisa?"

"But Mommy, I still see her." I don't know why I was surprised, but it seems I'm always caught off guard when I'm in the garden.

So I just said, "You can still see her? But how can that be? I don't understand."

Amy answered, "Oh Mommy, it's just that things are so different here. Sometimes I can see all of you. And Mommy, I know when you pray for me." Amy stopped all of a sudden and just sat down on the grass.

So I did the same and I became aware of how soft the grass felt. Then Amy looked up at me and said something that I would never forget.

"Mommy, I want to come home."

"Amy, oh Amy, don't you know how much we want that too!" . . . .

Then as so often happened when Lil was dreaming about Amy, she was suddenly wide awake and back in her own bedroom. She looked over at Peter who had sat up in bed, as if he knew that Lil had just come back from her heavenly journey.

He reached for her knowing she needed him. Then he said, "Do you want to talk about it?"

Lil nodded and began telling Peter about this last visit to the garden. Then she said, "Peter this time she told me plainly that she wants to come home."

Missy was awake early the next morning. She sat at the table eating her favorite cereal, oatmeal with brown sugar. She had very good manners. She put her napkin in her lap and didn't talk when her mouth was full. She was almost finished when she took a sip of juice and asked Debbie, "When can we go see Amy again?"

Debbie loved that her little girl had such a giving heart and that she wasn't the least bit put off by the machines that helped Amy to receive nourishment and monitored her heart and brain activity. It seemed that she wasn't even aware of them and yet when Missy had been on Amy's bed with her, you could tell she was being very careful not touch or move anything.

Debbie knew that Amy had always been able to breathe on her own and her heart was good. The doctors weren't sure why. Of course Lil said it was because of prayer and because of their loving Father.

Debbie had been so deep in thought that she had forgotten Missy's question, so Missy asked again, "Mama. When can we go see Amy again? I think she needs me."

Debbie smiled and said, "I'm not sure honey. I need to call Lil and see when we can work something out. I know you would like to spend time with her every day. We will just have to wait and see. Okay?"

Missy finished her cereal and drank the rest of her juice, wiped her mouth and then asked to be excused from the table. Then she looked up at her mama and said, "I'll try to be patient Mama, but it won't be easy."

Then she was off to her room to talk to her dolls and stuffed animals. The latest thing she was telling them or teaching them was about a man that had treated her so nicely in the garden. A man named Jesus. "Jesus helped me to come home," she told her captive audience. "So now we have to ask him to help Amy come home too. I think we should all pray for Amy again." Then with her head bowed and eyes closed Missy once again asked, "Jesus please help Amy to come home to her mommy and daddy real soon, cause they really need her. And so do I, cause she's my best friend. Thank you for helping. Amen."

Meanwhile, Lil has been on the phone, calling every prayer chain she could think of, because now she was convinced that there would soon be a breakthrough for Amy. In fact she was so convinced that this was going to happen she had called Gladys at home to tell her what was going on. She told her she needed to ask her something important.

Gladys was eager to help, "Lil what your tellin' me does sound like good news. I just knew you would be happy to hear about the monitor changin' and especially about when it happened. So please tell me what I can do to help you and Peter. You know I'll do anythin' I can."

"Yes Gladys, I do know that you are willing to help, but what I'm going to ask you is an awful lot to ask. What I'm thinking is when Amy wakes up I'm going to need help here at home. I will need someone trained in how to help . . . . It's hard for me to ask this, but Gladys I really think she will be coming back soon. And I want to know if you could come . . . ."

Gladys understood what Lil was trying to say, "Don't you worry yourself about anythin', the answer is yes! I will come and stay with you or I'll do whatever else is needed. Even though I would be willin' to bet that when Amy comes back she's goin' a surprise everyone."

Lil had tears in her eyes. She really wasn't surprised that Gladys would feel this way, but it still seemed a lot to ask. Then Lil said, "But what about the hospital. I don't want you to get in trouble there."

Gladys said, "Listen I have about three weeks of vacation comin', and they have been cuttin' my hours back some anyway. I'm sure we can work it all out. Besides I think even Doctor Gordman would be so happy to see Amy wake up, that he'd be willin' to put in a good word for me."

Lil was beyond tears now but she managed to respond, "Gladys I was sure I could depend on you. There is something special happening here between Amy and Missy. I have felt from the beginning that God had brought us all together, Peter and me with the Millers. But I had thought that it was for us to help them but now I'm not so sure. Now I'm beginning to think that it's the other way around and they've been sent to help us with Amy. I wish you could have seen Missy with Amy yesterday. She acts so mature and she is totally convinced that she's supposed to be there for Amy. Missy is so spiritual, it almost seems like she's an angel."

Gladys said, "Of course she's an angel and so is your Amy. They're all Gods little angels, because they are so close to Him."

David had called Peter to ask him if they could meet somewhere for lunch again, but it wasn't restaurant food he was after, it was spiritual food. David had got himself a new study Bible that was a little easier to read and he was absolutely devouring the gospels and the whole New Testament. That meant of course that he had more question.

So Peter suggested that they pick up hamburgers and head to the park. Once they had eaten their lunch Peter said, "Okay I'm ready. What's on your heart today, David?"

David said, "You know I'm going to have to start writing down my questions because I have so many, but today there are only two things that I would really like to cover."

Peter said, "Hum, only two, okay David go ahead and ask away."

David began, "One thing I would like to know about is water baptism. Should Debbie and I be baptized? And exactly what does it represent?"

Peter answered, "Yes, absolutely you should be baptized and usually I would have told you about it by now. It's just that things have happened so fast with you two and then with Missy coming home there just hasn't been a lot of time.

"As for what it represents, water baptism identifies us with Christ's death, burial, and His resurrection. In *Romans 6:4* Paul tells us, *(Therefore we have been buried with Him through baptism into death, in order that as Christ was raised from the dead through the glory of the Father, so we too might walk in newness of life.)* I would suggest that you both attend a class they have at the church. It covers all the scriptures in much greater detail than I can do here.

"I'm glad you brought it up, like I said I usually mention water baptism right away to people who have accepted Jesus. You and Debbie have come a long way very quickly and I couldn't be more pleased about that. Now I guess we're ready for the second question, you said you had two?"

David seemed reflective as they sat in the park, then he said, "This one is kind of tough. I hardly know how to ask you this. It's about Amy."

Peter's eyebrows shot up. David definitely had his attention. He said, "Okay David what is it you need to know about Amy that I haven't already shared?" Peter wasn't defensive but he was a little guarded. After all this was his daughter they were about to discuss and she and Lil were the most important people in his life.

David was aware that Peter was a little guarded and so he said, "Hey listen if I'm in any way, out of line here please tell me."

Peter just said, "I'll let you know."

So David went ahead and asked, "What, I wanted to ask you, because I just don't understand it. Why is it that you and Lil have so much faith and yet Amy is still in a coma? How can that happen?"

Peter looked a little strained but the question didn't surprise him. So he simply stated the truth. "Remember David, when I told you about the curse and about the enemy. His name is Satan and he is very real."

Peter could tell that what he had just said hadn't been what David had expected but he went on. "Now this is a subject that I have some understanding in, because Lil and I have had to do battle for two long years.

"First I want you to look at, *1 Peter 5:8* which tells us, *(Be of sober spirit, be on the alert. Your adversary, the devil, prowls about like a roaring lion, seeking someone to devour.)* But verse nine tells us that we are to resist the devil.

"And Jesus calls him the thief in, *John 10:10, (The thief comes only to steal, and kill, and destroy: I came that you might have life, and might have it abundantly.)*

"You see David, as long as we are here on this earth we will have to contend with the enemy. Lil and I do have faith, and we also have the Lord's promise, that He will never leave us or forsake us. So even though we haven't yet seen the total victory, we do see evidence of God's hand in our lives every day."

David had heard both Lil and Peter talk about the devil before, but now he realized that he hadn't been taking what they said all that serious. He finally spoke, "I'm sorry Peter. I know you have mentioned the devil or Satan before, but it obviously didn't sink in. I feel like I need to ask you to forgive me for being so ignorant."

Peter answered, "I think the world has painted the devil as some sort of cute little guy running around with a pitchfork for so long that most people don't believe that he exists. Even some churches pretty much ignore him. Which of course is a huge mistake? But then a lot of people don't even recognize the fact that we are spirit beings. So is it any wonder they don't understand spiritual warfare? David, don't worry that you have offended me. I'm not that thin skinned and the fact that you're asking about these things just shows me that you're interested in spiritual matters."

David picked up his Bible and said, "Thank you Peter, for straightening me out." He had written down the scriptures Peter used, so he could read them again and share them with Debbie.

They headed back to their cars. Peter stopped a minute, and said, "I want to thank you and Debbie for coming over the other night. Lil and I are convinced that Missy has a strong connection to Amy. I hope you will do it again soon that is if it doesn't upset Missy too much."

David had to laugh at that thought. He told Peter, "Are you kidding? She hasn't stopped putting pressure on us ever since we came over the last time. She just keeps asking us when she can go see Amy again."

Chapter Twelve

With all the excitement of having Missy home, David had pretty much forgotten all about trying to call Annabelle again. But now after hearing Missy talk about the garden he was more determined than ever to find out all he could about this book. So he was sitting in his car one afternoon after leaving school and trying her number once again. He had tried several other times but the number would just keep on ringing. David was about to hang up, when the phone was finally answered by a soft spoken woman who sounded very pleasant. David quickly responded, "Hello. Is this Annabelle Towns?"

"Why yes it is." Annabelle answered, from the other end of the line. "Who am I speaking with?"

David smile at the sweet voice, "Miss Towns, this is David Miller and I sent you an email a while back. I've been calling your number for quite some time, but . . . ."

"Mrs., its Mrs. Towns."

"Oh I'm sorry, Mrs. Towns, I meant no disrespect. I guess you caught me off guard, when you finally answered. I've been trying your number for some time now and . . . ."

"Oh it's perfectly all right; I'm not one to stand on formality anymore." She giggled, and said, "I guess you caught me off guard as well when you called me Miss Towns. Goodness, I haven't been called Miss since I married my late husband almost sixty years ago." She let out a sigh, as if she were remembering. I'm sorry I keep interrupting you, why don't you just call me Annabelle."

David just shook his head and thought, what an interesting lady. Then he went on to say, "Annabelle, it is then and you must call me David." Annabelle giggled again and David went on, "I'm calling about the book, *The Garden of Blessings".*

82

You remember that I sent you an email wanting to know more about the book?"

"Oh yes, of course I do remember. How I love that book. It belonged to my mother and then later she gave it to me. Then when I had my daughter, I would read it to her. It's a lovely book . . . ." Her voice trailed off as if she were reminiscing about a better time. "What would you like to know about the book? I just about have it memorized."

David said, "Could you tell me a little about the story line? You see, I'm not sure it's the book I'm looking for."

"The book was about a garden," Annabelle giggle again, "but of course you already know that from the title. There was a little girl that had a pet kitten. The author never gives the girl a name; he simply refers to her as Toby's mistress, because he wanted all the little girls that read the book, to pretend that they were that little girl. The author had written the book to educate children about all the little creatures that live in our gardens. Does that help?" Annabelle asked.

"You bet it does, Annabelle." David almost held his breath. Then he asked, "Do you still have the book?"

"No David, I'm so sorry. I wish I did, but we lost almost all of our personal possessions during a flood that ravished our farm back in nineteen sixty five. The book was ruined in that flood."

"Well, I can't say that I'm not disappointed, but at least I tried. You have been very gracious Annabelle, thank you for . . . ."

"Wait. I do know the whereabouts of two copies. You see that's why I went on the site, where you found my email. I was thinking that I would like to find a copy for myself. Actually there is only one owner that I was able to contact. Would you like that name and address?"

"Of course I would, but I thought you said that you wanted a copy."

"I did, but Miss Hollister wouldn't sell the book to me. She asked me all kinds of questions about myself and my family, but she just wouldn't sell me the book. She said she would know the right people, when they came along."

"Did she tell you why she refused you? Or what she was looking for?"

"No, she just said that the Lord would let her know."

David took the name and the address that Annabelle gave him. He thanked her for her help. David had meant to send a letter right away. However there was so much going on with Missy that he had put it off. He wanted the letter to be just right . . . . In fact, he wanted to write Patricia Hollister a letter that she couldn't refuse . . . .

For the next few days everyone pretty much got back to their routines, everyone that is except Missy. Her loyalty was daunting, she would pray each morning when she got out of bed and at every meal. She also prayed before her nap and naturally at bed time. What surprised Debbie the most was how often she would walk past Missy's room and see Missy in the process of positioning one of her dolls on their knees to pray.

Debbie admired her daughter's tenacity, but she also thought Missy might need a break. However, when she would try to get Missy to have one of her other friends over, Missy would tell her mother, "I will Mama, but not until Amy can be here too."

And so it was the first week went past with Missy spending as much time as could be arranged with Amy. By the second week, even though there was a great deal of love between the Iversons and the Millers, a certain amount of strain had developed.

During the second week Peter and David had gone to a game at the Middle School where David was a teacher. After the game they sat on the bleachers and David said, "There seems to be a little bit of tension between all of us lately and that worries me Peter. I sure don't want our friendship to end."

Peter knew what David meant. He had also become aware of the tension. He answered David, "Your right, I've noticed it too and I think I understand what is causing it. I believe that all of our expectations for Amy were really high, especially when we saw how Missy was with Amy. And there were all the things Missy told us about the garden and the angels. Everything she said lined up with Lil's dreams and we were all convinced that a break though was imminent. And now it's been almost two weeks since you first brought Missy over.

"I think that all of us are a little disappointed that we haven't seen something happen. For us Christians, this is always the hardest part about standing on our faith. It's also when we really have to get our backs up and not allow the devil to dissuade us."

David agreed at least in principle, but his concern was for Missy. He responded with, "I do understand what you're saying Peter, and I don't for one minute mean to suggest that we give up on Amy, but I have to admit that I'm a little concerned about Melisa.

"I'm not sure if you're aware that Debbie decided to home school Missy for a while, because she just didn't seem emotionally ready for regular school. She is so focused on praying for Amy that she has excluded almost every other activity from her life. I have to admit that I'm a little worried Peter. On one hand I admire Missy's spirituality so much, but on the other hand as her father it also frightens me a little."

Peter took what David told him very seriously. "David, I had no idea she was that absorbed with Amy. Perhaps we were wrong to have her over so much. I'll talk to Lil and perhaps we will need to back off a while."

David said, "That might be easier said than done, because Missy is one of the main reasons we've spent so much time at your place. She pretty much insists on spending as much time as she can with her and I'm quoting, 'Best friend'."

As the two fathers drove home they both were trying to figure out how to handle things. They both asked the Lord for His help. When they walked in through the kitchen everything seemed to be normal. They found their wives talking about the new fall fashions. Everything was as it should be . . . . Wasn't it?

Before long it was time to head home, so Debbie went to get Missy from Amy's room. She was surprised when she found Missy, not sitting on Amy's bed as usual, but she was sitting on the floor and she had big tears running down her checks.

Debbie went immediately to Missy and put her arms around her and asked, "Missy what is it sweetheart? What's the matter honey? Did something happen? But Missy just buried her head in Debbie shoulder and continued to sob.

Debbie picked up her weeping child and brought her out to the front room, where David was rounding up their coats. Everyone looked up with alarm and asked what was wrong. Debbie just shook her head and said, "I have no idea what has happened. I think for now we should just get Missy home. I'm sorry, but knowing Melisa she won't talk about this until she calms down. I'm sure she's not hurt or anything. I'm also pretty sure this is emotional. I'll call you and let you know what I find out."

After the Millers had left, Lil was real quiet and she looked worried. "Lil what is it? You've hardly said two words since the Millers left. Please tell me what's troubling you." Lil went to her husband just wanting to be held.

Then finally she said, "I think I know what upset Missy. I've felt it all evening. In fact I think we all felt it."

Peter looked up a little puzzled. He suspected that it had to do at least in part; with what he and David had discussed about the tension they were all feeling.

Lil, who was usually way ahead of her husband, walked into the kitchen and sat down at the table and pulled out a chair for Peter to join her. Then she said something that caught Peter totally off guard. "Peter I believe we are under a spiritual attack. I felt it all evening. Didn't you?"

Peter was surprised by what Lil had just said. He reached out and took Lil's hands, "Yes I was aware of the tension between all of us. In fact David and I discussed it when we were at the game. But an attack Lil, I don't know?"

Lil quickly answered, "Think about it Peter. Think of all the success we've had together with the Millers ever since we met them. They have both come to the Lord and little Melisa was given back to them. And Peter, you and I are more stirred up spiritually than we've been in months. And we're more convinced than ever that Amy will be given back to us and that she will be completely whole again."

Peter stood up, as he began to grasp what Lil was getting at. "Okay, I get your point. The devil can't stand all these victories, but surely not Missy."

Lil explained, "No, I don't think Missy is under an attack, but I do think she was overcome with disappointment. And she's very sensitive, so she most likely picked up on all the discouragement the devil was passing out to the rest of us."

"Okay Lil, I think you are more than likely right, as usual. So what are we going to do about it?"

Lil grinned at Peter and said, "I thought you would never ask. We bring out the big guns."

Peter just laughed. He knew that Lil was talking about sending up praise and worship to heaven, something the devil couldn't stand.

Lil no longer looked worried, now that she had a plan of action. She got up and put on a worship CD. "We need to call Debbie and David and share with them about what we've decided." And then she added, "I want to make sure we are all on the same page."

She said this as strains from the worship song floated in from the kitchen, (Oh we worship you our God, for you gave for us your life. Now we give back to you our lives in Jesus name. You gave the very best you had. Now Lord please help us do the same, in Jesus name.) Both Lil and Peter joined their voices with the music.

When they got home Melisa climbed out of the car under her own steam and literally marched into the house. She acted as if she was very upset. Actually it was more like she was angry with someone.

Debbie and David hadn't tried to find out what had upset Missy. They figured that she needed time to think about it, but they were sure puzzled by the way she was acting now.

Missy had gone straight to her room and was getting ready for bed when Debbie joined her. Debbie sat down on Missy's bed and said, "Do you want to talk about it? You know you can tell me anything."

Missy was scowling when she looked up at Debbie. Then the tears broke loose again and she threw both arms around her mother's neck and said through her tears, "Oh Mama I'm so mad at myself."

Debbie was totally mystified by what Missy said, so she asked, "I don't understand, sweetheart. Why are you mad at yourself?"

Missy tried to talk through her tear, "I . . . I got m-mad at Amy, I did Mama and I'm soo sorry. I love her so much."

Debbie rocked her daughter and said, "Of course you love Amy. Now tell me what happened."

Missy finally settled down enough that she could talk. "I got mad cause; I want Amy to be like she was in the garden. She was always so funny and she would always call me Sunny cause she said, I was like the sunshine. I don't understand Mama. I was so sure she was coming back. Why doesn't Jesus help her?"

By this time David had also come into the room and Debbie glanced up at him. Neither of them knew what to say. David decided to give it a try, "Honey your awful young to understand what's going on here, but when I asked Peter why Amy hadn't come back, he told me that we have an enemy called the devil and he's the one who has kept Amy from coming back. But Missy, he can't win any more, because we are all going to keep right on praying for Amy. And honey, I still believe that Jesus will help Amy because he loves you both so much."

Missy wiped her tears, "I'm so glad that Jesus isn't mad at me. Will you tell him I'm sorry?"

Debbie finally spoke up, "I'll bet you that Jesus already knows that you're sorry, and He also knows how much you care about Amy. So why don't we get ready for bed and then we will all get down on our knees and pray for Amy again. How does that sound?"

Missy hugged her mama and papa and then she grabbed her nightgown and ran into the bathroom. Missy's parents hoped that they had said the right things. They sure didn't want Missy to think that Jesus didn't love them.

While they were all getting ready for bed the phone rang. Debbie answered and it was Lil. She wanted to know how Missy was. Debbie explained how Missy had gotten discouraged and then how she got mad at herself and that was why she was crying.

Lil then went ahead and explained briefly to Debbie the conclusion that she and Peter had come to and what they plan to do about it. Then she had Debbie give the phone to David so he could hear the plan from Peter. David listened carefully to what Peter had to say and he thought, so this is spiritual warfare or at least one part of it.

After he hung up from his conversation with Peter he turned to Debra and said, "What do you think? It seems sort of simple to just praise. Peter gave me Isaiah 61:3. Is that what Lil told you?" Debra nodded.

Then David said, "Peter and I had talked earlier about the fact that there seemed to be some tension between all of us adults. Just now he suggested that it could be an attack of the enemy using discouragement, because we haven't seen the breakthrough we were all hoping for. I think it makes sense and Missy was definitely discouraged. I think we can trust Peter and Lil on this one. If anyone knows spiritual warfare it would be them."

Just then, in what had almost become the norm, another little voice was heard from, as Missy who didn't want to be left out asked, "What's spirit warfare?"

So her parents explained that the enemy they had talked about earlier didn't like hearing people sing praises to Jesus. Missy, who was always quick to catch on, gave her parents a big grin and said, "We should do it then, if the enemy doesn't like it. Isn't that right?"

Missy's parents felt very proud as they agreed, "Yes Missy that is right." Then in a few minutes a song taken right out of Isaiah 61:3 (KJV) rang out. Debbie with her lovely soprano voice was joined by Missy and David as they sang, "Put on the garment of praise for the spirit of heaviness, lift up your voice to God. Praise in the Spirit and the understanding, Oh magnify the Lord."

Missy woke bright and early the next day, even though they had gotten to bed quite late. By the time they sang praises and did some worship and of course they still had to get down on their knees to say a prayer for Amy. After all, Debbie had promised.

As Missy sat down at the table she announced, "I like doing spirit warfare and now I have something new to teach my dolls."

Debbie wasn't sure if Missy might be taking spiritual warfare a bit too lightly, but then she thought, she is only six years old.

On the other side of town Lil was also up early sitting with Amy, "You know about what is happening here don't you honey? Sweetheart, it's been far too long since I've had a dream about the garden. Oh Amy I hope you are aware of how much we want and need your precious spirit back in our lives. I don't know if you heard me calling after you, because I woke up right after you told me that you wanted to come home. You also told me that you know when we pray for you. So you must hear me all the time, because it seems to me that I have a prayer for you on my lips every minute of the day. I love you Amy, with all my heart." . . . .

Peter pulled into the lot at work. He had been listening to a worship CD on his way, he sat in the car for a while just thinking about Lil. He wasn't exactly worried about her but he was a bit concerned.

Lil, who was always strong in her faith, was still standing firmly on the word. The thing that concerned him was that there hadn't been any dreams for almost two weeks and that was unusual. He knew that Lil had been shook up when she woke from the last dream, when Amy had said plainly that she wanted to come home.

Lil had been so sure there would be a breakthrough that she had even called Gladys. She wanted her to be ready to help out when Amy woke up. "Dear God, please do something to let Lil know that Amy is aware of how much we want her with us. You have blessed us so much with the dreams and with little Missy and her parents. We thank you Lord, for this lovely family. Please just reveal yourself to Lil. Thank you Father. Amen."

David got home a little after three in the afternoon. As he came in through the back door Missy called out, "Mama, Papa's home."

David scooped Missy up in his arms and asked, "How's my favorite little prayer warrior?"

Missy planted a big kiss on her daddy's cheek and told him, "I'm okay, but I want us to pray for Aunt Lil, cause I think she is very sad."

Debra looked up from her dinner preparations shrugged her shoulders, as if Missy spiritual insight was always a mystery to her. David said, "So its aunt Lil now. When did this happen?"

Missy had climbed up in a chair so she could watch her mother make the salad. "Mama, do you think it would be okay if I call her Auntie Lil? I like her a lot and I feel really bad that she's so sad. I think she is very disappointed that Amy hasn't come back yet. That's why I want to pray for her."

Debbie stopped making the salad and picked up her little girl and said, "I'm sure that Lil wouldn't mind if you call her aunt Lil. And I think we should stop right now and say another prayer for her."

And so it was that there were prayers going up to heaven for Lil. Even Gladys had felt a strong urge to say a prayer for her dear friend, Lil Iverson. "Lord, I know she needs us to be prayin' for her, and it would sure be nice, if she would be gettin' one of those blessins'. Thank you dear Lord, Amen."

Chapter Thirteen

◆

The Garden of Blessings was filled with excitement. Today was the day when the angels came to pick up the blessings that the children brought to them. It was always very special to the children and they really enjoyed their part in the lovely ceremony.

Amy kept looking for her mother, but so far she hadn't seen her. She was one of the first in line to bring her blessing to one of the angels, so it was important that she stay put. Then she spotted her mom, she was just sitting down in her usual place on the white bench at the edge of the clearing. Amy waved her arms, but Lil didn't seem to notice her . . . .

I was watching all the children hurrying toward the place where they had met the angels before. I looked around trying to spot Amy but there was so much activity that I just couldn't find her. Then suddenly, I saw the beautiful beings again. I wanted to try and memorize how they looked so I could tell Peter what they were like, but they were so incredible that I couldn't come up with words to express what I was witnessing.

Just then, I saw Amy waving at me from across the field of blessings. I rose from the bench and began waving back at Amy. At that very moment, the angels stepped forward and began receiving the blessings from the children.

Amy gave one last wave, before she turned to follow the other children in her line, to deliver her blessing to an angel. Then I quickly lost sight of her. I waited by the bench for a while hoping Amy would come looking for me. It had helped me to see that Amy looked happy.

After a while when Amy didn't come, I got up and decided to walk down the path that Amy had taken the last time I had been here. I could smell the lovely fragrance of the lilacs. I was wishing that I had a way to tell Amy how much we wanted her home. And then something extraordinary happened . . . .

One of the beautiful beings stepped out from one of the lilac bushes, he bowed and then he handed me something that was sort of round and glowing. Then he bowed again and said, "I will tell Amy what you are feeling." As suddenly as he had come, he was gone.

I stood there holding the blessing. It felt soft in my hands, but it was glowing so much I wasn't quite sure what it was. I looked after the angel and called out my thanks. "Oh thank you, thank you so much . . . .

Lil was calling out her thanks, when she realized that she was waking up in the sun room where she had apparently fallen asleep. Lil was still calling out, "Thank you, thank you so much . . . ." Just as Peter came home from work and over heard her. He stepped into the sun room, just as Lil was rising from the sofa.

She was holding something in her hands. Lil's face was shining as she walked toward Peter and handed him the most lovely and fragrant lilacs he had ever seen. Peter took the lilacs from Lil, but he didn't speak. He understood that something truly special had just happened. He also sensed that Lil wasn't going to be able to share it, at least for a while.

He had seen his wife touched by heaven before, but never quite like this. They walked into the kitchen and Lil reached under the sink and brought out a large vase for the lilacs.

After putting the flowers in the vase, Lil carried them into Amy's room and set them across from her bed. They filled the room with their lovely scent. Lil walked over to Amy and bent down and kissed her on her cheek. "Thank you, dear Lord for this blessing." Then she and Peter went back to the kitchen, where she told him about her surprising visit to the Garden of Blessings.

Lil and Peter spent a quiet evening together, after Lil's incredible journey to the garden. Lil especially just wanted to savor what she had been given. They had gone into Amy's room several times to see if the lilacs were still there. The bouquet consisted of both purple and white blooms. Peter knew that it would be almost impossible to find lilacs in September.

Lil had wondered out loud, "Do you suppose the blessing that Amy gave to her angel was the same one that I received?

Peter considered the question before saying, "I don't think it matters Lil, it's all so supernatural. To me, what makes it so special is that you received the blessing while you were in the garden. If I didn't know how much you needed this, I just might be jealous. You do know don't you that you had a lot of people praying for you today?"

Lil said, "I did? . . . . No, I didn't know that."

Peter said, "Yep, I got a call from David and it turns out that Missy has given you the honorary title of aunt Lil. And it seems she has been concerned about you, because she thinks you are very disappointed that Amy hasn't come back yet. She said she knew how you felt, because she had felt the same way. Then she insisted that they all pray for you.

"And then after that Gladys called me to find out how you were doing and to tell me that she had been praying for you too. So there were a lot of people interceding for you, including me. And that's simply because we all love you so much."

Lil put her head down on her husband's shoulder. Tears filled her eyes as she answered, "You all knew how much I needed the support right now. I'm so fortunate to have all of you in my life."

Long after the Iversons had gone to bed, there remained a soft glow around the bouquet of lilacs. And if you watched carefully you just might see a slight smile on Amy's face.

The next morning, Debbie called Lil to see how she was doing. Lil told Deb she had something very unusual to share with her and Missy so she invited them over for lunch. The answer heard through the telephone receiver from Missy was a very loud "Yes!"

At Eleven o'clock Missy and Debbie arrived at Lil's door. They were ushered in and taken directly to Amy's room and shown the beautiful bouquet of lilacs.

Missy was very excited to tell aunt Lil, all about how they had prayed for her and how much she liked doing (spirit warfare).

"I just knew that God would answer our prayers." Missy beamed. "See Mama, I was right. Jesus still loves us," and then more quietly she asked, "Auntie Lil can I please have one of the lilacs to put in Amy's hair?"

Lil was pleased to see Missy's faith being rewarded. She took some scissors and cut a bloom for each of the girls. "Oh thank you, I love them. And then she climbed onto Amy's bed and put one of the flowers in Amy's hair.

As Debbie and Lil sat in the sun room, Lil told her about how much the trip to the garden had meant to her this time. "I think I really needed this so I would know that Amy wasn't unhappy and then the angel told me he would tell Amy what I was feeling. Just think about that Debbie, the angel knew what I had just wished for. So even though I didn't get to talk to her, I'm sure she is aware of how much we want her home. It's hard to believe that for almost two years I took it for granted that she knew how much we wanted her back. How could I have done that?"

Debbie said, "Lil, from everything you've told me about Amy, I don't think she would have ever doubted that you wanted her home. I'm sure she would have known. Surely she knew how much you both love her."

Lil didn't have to think about what Debbie said for very long before she answered, "You're right, of course she knew. Then why was I feeling so guilty?"

Debbie cocked her head to one side and frowned, "Oh come on Lil you know the answer to that better than I do. Who is the one that puts doubt, guilt and fear on us?"

Lil had to laugh at herself, because Debbie the student was teaching the teacher. Lil just nodded and said, "No matter how long you've been a Christian there are still times when you need support from others. Thank you Debbie."

They got up and went into the kitchen where Lil had prepared some sandwiches and hot tea. Missy came and joined them just long enough to eat a sandwich, before she headed back to her post beside Amy.

Chapter Fourteen

Gladys had the day off. She had done her shopping early and had worked for a while in her tiny garden. It was truly small, but Gladys thought, "I love it just the way it is; I wouldn't have time to keep anythin' any bigger." She had a lilac bush and some bleeding hearts that would bloom in the spring. She had several hanging pots that held winter pansies and some golden mums and she even grew a few strawberries. "Yes, this is just right for me," she smiled to herself.

She went back inside and decided to give Lil a call. She had been a little concerned about her dear friend, even though Lil was a strong woman, everyone needed a bit of a boost now and then.

"Good afternoon," was the reply that came across the telephone lines.

"Well you sound pretty chipper," said Gladys, "I guess I don't have to worry about you anymore."

Lil knew the voice instantly and quickly responded, "According to Peter I had a lot of support from my very dear friends. He told me that both you and David had called yesterday to say that you were praying for me. I must tell you those prayers were answered in a most astonishing way."

Gladys was almost as excited to hear how the Lord had worked in Lil's life as Missy had been. "That is so wonderful Lil and you're tellin' me that you actually have those lilacs in Amy's room. Oh what a sight that must be, to have lilacs from heaven. My goodness Lil, I can hardly take it all in. I did ask the good Lord to please send you one of those blessins'. I can't tell you how thrilled I am for you. Your news has just made my day!"

Lil was tickled as she went on talking to her dear friend, "You know Gladys, I think you might even be more excited than Missy was. And I thought she was going to bust a button.

She was so happy to know that Jesus wasn't mad at her, even though she had gotten upset."

Lil went on to explain how Missy had been discouraged and she knew that Lil was feeling the same. "I must say, I can't think of a better group of people to have praying for me than all of you. Thank you Gladys you're a dear friend and your welcome to come see the lilacs for yourself."

After Gladys hung up, she didn't think she could be any happier and then the doorbell rang. She went to answer it and this time she was speechless.

Her handsome son stood there with his blond hair freshly trimmed. And he wasn't alone; he had with him a lovely young woman with long brown hair. When Raymond realized that his mother wasn't going to speak, he stepped forward and said, "Mom I would like you to meet Tracy. She's the girl I told you about."

Gladys pulled herself together and took the young women in her arms to welcome her. Then she finally said, "I am truly happy to meet you." She invited them in and got them settled on the couch, before she went to make some coffee to go with the apple turnovers she had just taken from the oven.

Ray was telling Tracy, "You haven't lived until you've had one of Mom's apple turnovers. You're going to love them." Tracy was happy to see that Ray was showing his mother respect. She truly loved her mother and felt very strongly that mothers should be treated right.

Gladys came in carrying a tray which Ray immediately took from her and sat it on the coffee table. Gladys served them each a cup of coffee and a turnover.

Tracy spoke up, "Thank you Mrs. Tanner, these are delicious. I've been after Ray to bring me over to meet you. When I first met Ray he had told me that you and he were on the outs. He said he felt bad about that, so I simply told him that he needed to do whatever he could, to fix things between you."

Gladys nodded her head, "Raymond did tell me all about that Tracy and he's been doin' just that. He came over and stayed with me a few days and he told me that he wanted to fix everythin' between us. He even went with me to church and rededicated his life to the Lord. And I must say that I give you a lot of the credit for that, but then of course, there are the blessins'."

Apparently Ray had told Tracy about what had gone on at the hospital, so she wasn't surprised when Gladys brought up the blessings. They talked for a while longer. Then Ray went to the store to get a few things his mom needed to make her special spaghetti sauce for dinner.

"I'm so glad you agreed to stay for supper, it gives us a chance to get better acquainted. You know my son thinks very highly of you, and so do I. Raymond never had a girlfriend that he was willin' to straighten out his life for and I couldn't be more pleased."

Tracy smiled; she was happy that Ray's mother seemed to like her. "Please don't give me too much credit. Ray was already feeling very repentant by the time we met. So I just gave him a little push. He told me that his Mama had taught him right. So he knew that it was just a matter of time, before he would have to get right with God."

Gladys took Tracy's hands and said, "Thank you child, you don't know how much that means to me." . . . .

After they had eaten and cleaned up the dishes. Raymond said, "Wow Mom, I think you may have outdone yourself today. Between the turnovers and that dinner I am absolutely stuffed."

"Yes, Mrs. Tanner that was a great meal. I think it might be the best spaghetti dinner I've ever had." Then Tracy added, "I'm serious. No wonder Ray wanted to get things fixed up between you."

That got a chuckle out of Gladys. And then she went on and shared with them about little Missy and how they were all believing that Amy would soon be awake too. Then she told them how Lil had asked her if she would come to help out when the time came.

Tracy looked up with excitement and said, "I just knew it. I knew there was more to my meeting you, other than the fact that your Ray's mother. I have felt all day that God was doing something special here. Now I think it has something to do with Amy."

Gladys looked puzzled and said, "What is it child? What are you thinkin'?"

Ray caught on just then and gave Tracy a broad grin. Then Tracy explained to Gladys, "You see Mrs. Tanner, I'm a physical therapist and I'm out of a job right now, because the Lord told me He was sending me a special patient."

Gladys began to nod and then she said, "Oh dear Lord, what are you fixin' to do?"

Chapter Fifteen

Melisa was outside with a few of her dolls. Debbie had finally convinced her that her dolls needed some fresh air. It was the first time she had agreed to play outside since she had come home.

Debbie was very proud of Missy's tenacity regarding her new found faith and her determination to be there for Amy. Missy had announced, "I won't give up on Amy, cause she has to come back so we can be best friends forever."

Debbie looked out the window and was happy to see the little girl from across the street playing with Missy on the swings. She took them out some refreshments and Missy introduced her to Vicky Marie . . . .

Once Vicky Marie had gone home, Missy asked, "Mama what is my middle name?"

Debbie told her that her middle name was Anna. Missy frowned and then she said, "From now on I want to be called Melisa Anna, cause it's a more grownup name."

Debbie said, "I suppose this came from your new friend, since she has a double name."

Missy said, "She told me that Missy is a baby's name. So I decided to be called Melisa, but just to make sure I think I should be called Melisa Anna." With that out of the way, Melisa, went back to her room.

At about two o'clock the doorbell rang and it was Vicky Marie, "Hello, could I please come in and play with Melisa?"

"Yes of course, she's in her room. Let me just show you."

After Debra took Vicky Marie to Melisa's room she called David to tell him what was going on. David had to laugh when he heard that Missy insisted on being call Melisa Anna. "That's going to be hard to remember, but I guess if it's what she wants then we need to try."

When David got home at about five, Melisa came out of her bedroom to greet him. "Papa I played outside today."

David sat down in his easy chair in the front room and said, "I understand you are to be called Melisa Anna, now that you are growing up."

Melisa hung her head down, a reaction that usually meant she was unhappy about something. David looked over at Debbie, who seemed surprised by this reaction.

Debra asked, "What is it Melisa? Did something happen?"

Missy looked up with a stern look on her face and said, "I've changed my mind, I'm still going to be Missy." And with that she gave her dad a kiss and then headed back to her room.

David looked totally confused, "I thought you told me she had insisted."

Debbie shook her head, "I guess I better go find out what has happened." Debbie went into Missy's room and found her daughter sitting in the middle of her bed. She wasn't crying, but she sure looked unhappy. Debbie asked, "Honey did something happen to make you unhappy?"

Missy scooted to the edge of the bed and patted the mattress beside her, indicating she wanted her mother to join her. "Mama we were playing church and one of the dolls got sick. I told Vicky Marie that we needed to do spirit warfare and she didn't know what that was. I tried to explain to her that we're new Christians and that I have a friend that's sick and we do spirit warfare for her. She still didn't know what I meant, so I asked her if she was a Christian. She said yes, they go to church some of the times. Then I tried to tell her about the garden and the angels, but then she said she had to go home. I don't think she likes me Mama."

Debbie realized that this was their first experience with someone having trouble understanding their new faith. "Oh Missy, it isn't you. Some people just don't understand the supernatural. I guess when we meet new people we just have to be a little careful about sharing our faith."

Missy looked up at her mother and said something very profound, "But Mama, it's what's important!"

"Yes Missy, you're absolutely right. It is what's important!"

It had been several days since Lil's visit to the garden, but she told Peter that she was okay and she was prepared to wait. The way she had put it was, "I'm prepared to stand and keep on standing."

So when the Millers came over on Friday evening for Bible study. Lil shared the scriptures in Ephesians 6:10-18. She showed them where it talks about how we wrestle not against flesh and blood. Then they talked about the need to put on the whole armor of God.

Peter gave a quick summary of the armor, *(Gird Your Loins with Truth, and there is the Breastplate of Righteousness, and of course you have the Gospel of Peace. There's the shield of faith and the Helmet of Salvation. Last but not least you have the sword of the Spirit, which is the <u>word</u> of God).* Peter said, "Now this is how we prepare for spiritual warfare."

Missy piped up and said, "Some people don't understand spirit warfare and then they get mad and go home." All eyes were on Melisa as they wondered where this had come from.

Then Debbie explained about Missy's experience with her little friend Vicky Marie. And they were all very impressed with Missy's conclusion of what was important.

Lil said, "I'm very proud of you Missy, I think you're very good at spiritual warfare."

Missy nodded and said, "Yeah, I think I am. Aren't I Mama?" Everyone got a kick out of that.

David told Lil and Peter that they were all going to be baptized this weekend. "All three of us will be going forward and then we will all be baptized."

Peter said, "Hey, that's good news. It's hard to believe we've only known each other for a few weeks. You've all come such a long way."

Lil got up to take something to the kitchen and when she turned on the light she realized that Missy had followed her. She put her arm around Missy, and asked, "Did you want something sweetheart?"

Missy nodded and said, "Auntie Lil, I wanted to wait to be baptized so Amy could be there too, but Mama wants all of us to be baptized at the same time."

Lil was always impressed by Missy sweet spirit. She answered her carefully. "Missy that's very nice of you, but even if Amy woke up right away, it would probably take a while before she could go to church. So, why don't you go ahead and get baptized with your mom and dad. And then you can tell Amy all about it. Would that be okay?"

Missy said yes, that would be alright and then she skipped back to the front room. Lil couldn't help thinking what a wonderful twosome Missy and Amy were going to make . . . . That evening, Lil told Amy that she had done a very good job of picking out a best friend. What a wonderful combination they would make. Lil thought, "They will really complement each other."

Sunday the Millers were baptized and Missy got to meet a few other children that knew what (spirit warfare) was all about. So now she could at least talk about it with someone.

When Missy shared the day with Amy, she told her, "I guess nobody can really understand unless they've been to the garden. I miss you Amy, please hurry home. I'm doing spirit warfare as best as I can."

Lil hadn't meant to eavesdrop, but she had come to tell Missy that her dessert was waiting for her. Then she had overheard the little girl's plea and the tears had just popped out uninvited.

She had quietly backed down the hall and ducked into the bathroom to plash some water on her face. It truly did seem that Melisa was the only one who really understood how hard it was. Partly because they had both been with Amy recently and they had seen her, the way she should be. They had been with the Amy that was funny and that could be such a clown and yet was also such a caring little girl.

Lil sent up a silent prayer, "Oh God I'm sorry. Just when I think I'm doing fine, then something else happens and I almost lose control." Lil dried her face and stepped out of the bathroom.

Missy was waiting. She looked up into Lil's teary eyes and then threw her little arms around Lil's middle and said, "I'm sorry Auntie Lil, I know what you're going through."

"Oh sweetheart, I think you do. Because you know just how special our Amy is."

Another week had passed without any real changes except, the lilacs had faded. All the people that were close to the Iversons had taken at least one bloom to press into a book. They knew that only a few people would believe that they were from a heavenly garden, but the Iversons and the Millers knew.

Lil continued to design the dresses that would be made up, to sell in her shop. Peter went on selling businesses and homes. David kept up his teaching and coaching at the Middle School. Debbie continued home schooling Melisa and she also got more involved at the church, helping out where she was needed.

Then of course little Missy kept up her spirit warfare. She was ever vigilant. Watching carefully for any change in her best friend's condition . . . .

Peter and Lil still saw a lot of Debbie and David. They continued doing the evening Bible studies together. While Missy sat and talked to Amy and shared all she was learning from her mother, for the first grade. Both families continued to pray for Amy to come home soon.

It was after one of these evenings that I woke up in the garden. I could smell the lilacs and I heard some children laughing. I saw Amy playing with a group of children, but as soon as she saw me, she hurried over. She asked me, "Did you like the lilacs?"

I nodded, I was so happy to see her I couldn't talk for a minute, then I said, "I loved them, they were heavenly."

We both laughed at that. And then we began walking down a path, until we came to a fountain. Amy said, "Can you guess where we are?

I shook my head and said, "No I don't know, please tell me."

"We're at the fountain of blessings. I especially love it here. I like to listen to the music it makes. Can you hear it?"

I listened carefully for a while, until I heard what sounded like babies making cute little gurgling sounds. "What is it Amy? What am I hearing?" I asked.

Amy was grinning, "Those are the sounds of little baby spirits and they will be given to very special people. Listen, did you hear that one? That's a little baby boy. And guess what? I know where he's going."

I knew Amy was teasing me and I got all excited. Amy did that to people. I said, "Oh Amy, tell me where is he going and when?"

Amy looked very serious, "You'll never guess . . . . I think in about Eight months, let me see now. He will be going to . . . . Oh yes, he will be going to the Millers."

I asked her, "Which Millers? Amy, please tell me."

Amy, always the clown said, "Okay if you insist," and she bowed with a flourish, and said, "He's going to David and Debbie."

I was so surprised I didn't know what to say. I was about to ask her more questions . . . .

When Amy suddenly looked up, and said, "Oh I have to go right away. I have to go to the field of blessings, because someone is going home." Amy turned and ran off toward the field. I stood there watching her run across the field . . . . And then I woke up with a start . . . .

I was calling out, "Mama, Papa come quickly. Mama, I had a dream."

Debbie and David woke up hearing Missy crying out. They jumped out of bed and ran to Missy's room. She was standing up in her bed. David took her into his arms. They were both checking her over to see if she was hurt.

"Mama, she's coming home. Amy is coming home. Please call Auntie Lil, she will need her mommy. Amy will need her."

David and Debbie didn't know what was happening. Finally Debbie got her voice and asked, "What do you mean Missy? Please tell us what happened."

Missy went from David into Debbie's arms. "I'll tell you Mama. But please, you have to call Auntie Lil, so she can be with Amy." Debbie nodded for David to go ahead and make the call. She knew he would try to explain why they were calling in the middle of the night.

Then Debbie went over to a chair and sat down with Missy. "Okay honey, your dad is calling aunt Lil. Now please tell me what this is all about."

Missy said, "Mama, I was dreaming that I was in the garden with Amy. We were laughing just like we used to. And then she told me that she had to go to the field of blessings, cause someone was going home. Oh Mama, as I watched her run across the field, I saw two angels go to Amy and take her to the same place where they took me when I was sent home." . . . .

Peter woke to the sound of the phone ringing. He reached for it and answered, "Hello." He sat there listening to what the caller said, "What, she what? Is Missy okay? I don't know? Wait a minute David."

Lil was up watching Peter trying to figure out what was going on. Peter covered the receiver, and said, "Apparently Missy had a dream about the garden and she insisted that they call you so you could be with Amy. And Lil, Missy said to tell you that Amy's coming home." . . . .

By that time David had taken Missy back from Debbie and had handed Debbie the phone. Debbie came on the line and said, "Peter why don't you give the phone to Lil and I will try to explain what happened."

Lil took the wireless phone from Peter and while she listened, she hurried into Amy's room. They kept a small lamp on all night. When Lil entered her daughter's room everything seemed the same. Lil told Debbie, "Okay Debbie, tell Missy I'm in Amy's room and I'll stay right here. And tell her I said thank you."

Lil sat down on the edge of Amy's bed and spoke, "Sweetheart can you hear me? Missy says your coming home and I believe her. Oh Amy, I believe you have a special connection with Missy. I remember when you talked about her the first night she was in the hospital. You knew about her before I did.

"Remember you told me that she was a little frightened, so you would be spending a lot of time with her. Missy is so loyal to you and she has told me things about the garden, things that I saw in my dreams."

Lil hesitated and then went on, "Honey, I saved you some of the lilacs; they are pressed in our family Bible. I love you sweetheart, but you've always known that."

Lil looked at Peter, who had joined her and was now standing next to Amy's bed. Lil finally asked, "What time is it?"

Peter told her, "It's nearly five o'clock. I guess we may as well stay up." He sat down in a chair and then added, "I went ahead and started the coffee. Did you find out anymore from Debbie?"

Lil explained to Peter, "Apparently Missy had a dream about the garden. And in the dream she had been talking to Amy when Amy said she had to go because someone was going home. Missy told Debbie that as she watched Amy run across the field, two angels came and took Amy to the same place they had taken Missy when she was sent home."

Peter got excited about what he heard, "Wow Lil, I think we have to believe this. We already know there's a powerful connection between Missy and Amy."

Lil got up and went over and turned on another light, then she looked at the monitors but they showed no change. She turned and looked at Peter and said, "I don't think we can expect the monitors to tell us what's going on, because this is totally supernatural. I think we should just watch Amy. She will let us know when she is back."

Peter agreed with Lil, "Why don't you stay with Amy, and I'll go get us some coffee and I should probably call David back. I guess Missy was beside herself with worry that Amy would wake up without you by her side."

Lil was brushing the hair back from Amy's face, "Thanks Peter, I could use some coffee. Yes, please do call them and be sure to have them tell Missy thank you. She is such a special little girl. And also tell them that we will let them know at the slightest change."

After talking with Peter, David hung up the phone, "That was Peter, he asked me to tell Missy thank you, and he also said that they will call us as soon as there is any change."

Missy was at the table having her cereal, she said, "They have to watch Amy really close . . . . Maybe they need me to help."

David chuckled at his daughter, she knew a little about how to work people. "I think that between Lil and Peter, they should be able to watch one little girl."

Missy wanted so much to be with Amy, "I know Papa but nobody else knows Amy like I do. I would know better what to look for."

Debbie, who was listening to the banter between father and daughter, had to smile at her daughter's tenacity. "Missy, I will call Lil this afternoon and I'll let you talk to her. Will that be okay?"

"Okay Mama, I'll just go do some more spirit warfare. I'll bet that will help Amy." With that said Missy hopped down from her chair and headed for her room where she had all her dolls and stuffed animals lined up ready to do battle.

After hearing Peter teach on the Christians armor, Missy had tied ribbons around her dolls to represent the girding with truth and then she had cut out shields and swords, so they were all ready to do spirit warfare. Missy got her new picture Bible out and got down on her knees. A minute later as Debbie walked past her daughter's room she was reminded of the scripture in Luke.

> *Luke 18:16, But Jesus called for them saying,*
> *"Permit the children to come to Me,*
> *And do not hinder them,*
> *For the kingdom of God belongs to such as these."*

Chapter Sixteen

◆

Amy turned away from Missy and started running to the field of blessings. She didn't want to miss anything. She was about half way across the field when two of the heavenly beings came up to her, one on each side. They were so beautiful and filled with light like a rainbow.

The one on Amy's right leaned down and said very softly, "Amy we have been sent to tell you to come with us. For Amy, it is you, who is going home."

Amy was almost speechless but she got her voice quickly, "Thank you so much. Could I please just take a rose to my Mommy?"

The angel on the other side of Amy said, "There isn't enough time. We need to hurry."

Amy felt like her feet didn't even touch the grass as the angels hurried her to the place by the trees. It was the place where they always took the children who were going home.

Everyone was there. They were calling out to her and telling her goodbye. Others were sending good wishes. Amy waved and blew kisses to everyone. The first angel bent down again and pressed something into Amy's left hand, then he put his hand on top of her head and said, "Goodbye little one, goodbye Amy." . . . .

Amy's eyes felt very heavy and she felt herself floating, just floating away. The children were calling, "We love you Amy. We all love you."

Amy was thinking about the beautiful beings as she floated along she could hear the garden sounds fading away. The children's voices began to fade in and out and then she heard the birds singing, fading . . . . fading away. And she began to hear other sounds as she drifted in and out. Amy heard someone singing, or maybe it was a music box. She couldn't quite make it out . . . .

And then she heard something else . . . . Something she loved more than anything. "I love you Amy. Sweetheart, you know how much we both love you." . . . .

Then Amy felt something . . . . Someone was brushing her hair back from her face, and it felt so good . . . .

"Ummom . . . . Ummom . . . ."

Lil sat on Amy's bed brushing the hair back from her face and telling her how much they love her. Then she heard it. It sounded like humming. Amy was trying to talk.

"Peter, come quickly. Yes darling, I can hear you. What are you trying to say?"

"Momm, momm."

Lil with tears streaming down her cheeks answered, "Yes Amy it's your Mommy."

By now Peter was there too. He was bending over Amy and he too had tears flowing freely. "Amy, it's your Daddy, we are both here sweetheart."

Amy's eyes were open now, as she tried to focus. "Daaddee, momm, anngel." Lil went and got a wash cloth and wiped Amy's face. Amy said, "Goodd, ful goodd."

Peter was overcome with joy and started dancing around. "Daaddee funnee. Wan wha ter." Lil was up in an instant to get Amy some water. Lil lifted her head just a bit. She could only take a sip, but it was a start.

"Wan Milsee, misss."

Peter said, "Honey, are you asking for Missy?"

"Yes, wan Milsee."

Peter got up and made the call. He told Debbie that Amy was awake and she was asking for Missy. After he hung up, he told Lil, "Needless to say, they will be right over."

Amy was trying to lift her head. Lil took a pillow and helped her to sit up a little. Then she took more water. "Anngel, homme."

Lil caught on and said, "Did the angels help you come home?"

"Yes I gaarden milsee, I com hom. So hoppee mommee. War daddee?"

Lil told Amy that her daddy was making some calls. Peter was letting Gladys know that Amy was awake. He came back in the bedroom, "Gladys will be over in about two hours." He looked at his daughter. He was still shedding tears of joy.

Amy said, "Wy daadee crii?"

"Honey those are tears of joy for you."

Amy seemed to get stronger each minute. "Mommee wan ice criim."

Peter laughed and said, "Why not Lil? I don't think a little taste of ice cream will hurt her. Besides we have to remember that this is all supernatural."

Lil laughed and went to get Amy a little ice cream.

David and Debbie had stopped to pick up some sweet rolls on the way to the Iverson's house. Missy could hardly contain her excitement. "I knew Amy would need me, cause I was with her right before she came home. Hurry Papa, I can't wait any longer."

Debbie thought she should try and warn Missy that even though Amy was awake she was having a little trouble talking. Debbie told Missy, "Honey you do understand that Amy was in a coma for a long time. She is talking some, but Peter said she is having a little trouble with her speech."

Missy still squirming around in the back seat said, "I know Mama, but remember I knew what Amy wanted, even when she couldn't talk."

David chuckled. "She's got you there Deb. I'm beginning to think our daughter is way ahead of us adults when it comes to spiritual matters."

They rounded the corner to the Iversons and pulled up into the driveway. Missy was out of the car and half way to the door, before her parents even got their doors open.

Peter opened the front door to receive Missy, "Hello Mr. Iverson, I bet you're really happy."

Peter said, "Yes Missy, we are very happy. Thank you for telling us about Amy."

Missy answered, "I knew she would need her mommy. May I please go see her now? I just can't wait any more."

Peter moved to the side to let Missy go past and she was up the stairs to Amy's room in a flash. Lil heard her coming and met her at the door, "Hello Missy, there is someone here really looking forward to seeing you."

Amy was propped up a little more now. When she saw Missy, she said, "Low Sunee Milsee, I hoppee seee yuu."

Missy usually the proper little girl, squealed and said, "Amy, you remembered what you called me. I've missed you so much. I brought my music box with our song on it. And Amy, I saw the angels come for you, so I knew you were coming home. And I woke everyone up to tell them."

Amy said, "Way too goo, Milsee."

Missy squealed again and said, "Oh Amy, I'm so glad that you're back."

Lil met Debbie out in the hall. "All I can say to anyone who doubted Missy's story about meeting Amy in the garden, is they would have to change their minds if they witnessed what I just did. Debbie, it's so obvious that they already know each other."

Debbie gave Lil a big hug and then she just held on. "I am so very happy for you. I knew when Missy said, that she saw the angels take Amy to the same place they had taken her. I just knew that it was going to happen. Lil, after all the waiting, there just aren't enough words to express the happiness I feel for you right now. You and Peter really deserve this."

Lil who was grinning and crying, answered, "Don't we have some really remarkable little girls?" They were both crying now as they heard the strains of (Yes, Jesus loves Me.) coming down the hall from Missy's music box.

Lil smiled as Debbie leaned into Amy's room to just watch the girls for a few minutes. They were doing just fine.

Then Peter called up to them, "Hey you ladies want to join us for coffee and some sweet rolls?"

They settled around the table in the kitchen. All of their faces were shining, both with tears and with joy. They all took hands and sent a truck load of thanks and praises to heaven for reuniting Amy with her parents.

As they finishing up the coffee the doorbell rang. Peter opened the door to find Gladys standing there carrying an overnight bag. And there was a lovely young woman with her. Peter said, "Gladys, thanks for coming."

Gladys came through the door smiling and talking, "Are you kiddin*'" me I wouldn't be anywhere else. I am so happy I was on cloud nine all the way over here. Now, I'd like to introduce you to a friend of Raymond's."

Lil had joined them and Gladys explained how Tracy was a physical therapist and how the Lord told her, He was going to give her a very special patient.

"Oh Gladys, the Lord just thinks of everything. Thank you." Then Lil turned to Tracy and thanked her for coming. "Now let's go upstairs, so you can meet Amy."

When they entered her room, Amy's eyes lit up. Amy seemed to recognize Gladys. "Low I member yu. Yu always say ga morn nee mee."

Gladys went over to Amy and opened up a little box and presented her with another music box. "Now both of my little angels have a music box of their very own."

Gladys had tears, as she introduced Tracy to Amy. Tracy said, "I think it would be pretty safe to say, that this is the happiest group of people I've ever seen."

Lil showed Gladys where she would be staying, in the room right next door to Amy.

Then a little later Missy came and got Lil. "Auntie Lil, come and look at what Amy has. She has something to give to you."

And sure enough Amy held out her left hand, and when she opened it there was a beautiful white feather, "Angel giv to me for Mommee."

Lil took the feather from Amy, "Oh Lord my heart is so full, that I can hardly take it all in. How will I ever be able to give you enough thanks? Thank you for all the gifts, but especially for returning these adorable little girls. Thank you Lord, again and again!"

It was easy to convince Missy that Amy needed to rest but she was absolutely sure she needed to stand guard. She finally agreed to go home when Lil promised to call her if Amy needed her.

Lil was tired, but she also knew she was way too high with emotions to be able to sleep. Gladys had offered to sit with Amy so Lil could get some rest. Lil said, "Thank you Gladys, you know that I trust you but I can't settle down, not just yet."

Peter had gone to their room to try and get a little rest. He dozed off, giving thanks to God for His grace.

At about two o'clock, the doorbell rang again and when Lil answered, she was surprised to see Dr. Gordman. "Hello Lil, I hope it's alright for me to stop by. Gladys called me as soon as she knew that Amy had awakened."

Lil opened the door wider and stepped back as she said, "Of course it's alright, please come in. I'm afraid Amy tired herself out a bit. There's been so much excitement, between seeing Gladys and the Millers. And then of course there's little Missy. Amy slept for a couple of hours, but you know Doctor Gordman, it's just so different from the coma. Now she stirs when we walk into the room."

Dr. Gordman was watching Lil, "Mrs. Iverson I can't begin to tell you how happy I am, to be proved wrong. I have always been impressed with you and your husband's faith. It makes me want to meet the person, behind that kind of faith."

Peter, who had gotten up when he heard the doorbell, stepped forward and welcomed Dr. Gordman and then he said, "You know that could be arranged, we are always ready to share."

Dr. Gordman nodded, and then he said, "Can you tell me how it happened, how Amy woke up?" Peter and Lil took Dr. Gordman into the living room and told him all about Missy's dream and the incredible story of Amy's return.

Dr. Gordman seemed a little stunned at the story he was told, but he said, "If it was coming from anyone else besides you, I might have trouble believing this. But since it's coming from the two of you, I have to say I do believe it. Now if it would be alright, I would love to go see this miracle."

Amy was awake and listening to the music box, that Gladys was gladly rewinding for her. Gladys stood up as the doctor entered the room. She beamed a smile his way, and said, "Good afternoon Doctor, I knew you would want to see for yourself, what was goin' on at the Iversons. It's a miracle, no doubt about that."

Dr. Gordman came into the room and smiled at Amy, and said, "I am so very pleased to meet you Amy. How are you feeling?"

Amy smiled up at the doctor and answer, "Beter ever minnit, than you."

Dr. Gordman asked Lil if it would be alright if he examined Amy, which he did. Then when he got up to leave he said, "Amy I want you to know that you have amazing parents. I truly believe it was their faith that brought you back."

Amy said, "I kno it was!" And then she gave him a big smile, as he left the room.

Down stairs he told Lil that Gladys could unhook the monitors. "I continue to be amazed by Amy. And Mrs. Iverson I want you know this is a bona fide miracle. I hope you'll let me know if you need anything, anything at all."

Then when Peter walked him to the door, the doctor said, "Peter I was serious about wanting to meet the person behind your faith."

Peter shook his hand and assured him, that he would be happy to meet with him. And then he told him, "You're already way ahead of most people, because you recognize the fact that our faith is in the person, of Jesus Christ."

"Yes, I do know that."

After they said their goodbyes and Peter closed the door he said, "Dear Lord, this whole thing just keeps growing."

He went upstairs and to share the news with everyone. He told them, "Dr. Gordman, says he is serious about meeting the person behind our faith and he knows that person is Jesus."

Amy clapped her hands and said, "Jesus good."

Everyone responded with, "Yes Amy, Jesus is very good."

On the day that Amy had come home, Lil had taken Peter's hand. They had gotten down on their knees next to their daughter's bed and together they had thanked the Lord from the bottom of their hearts for bringing Amy back to them. They had stood on God's promises for two long years and now they knew that they would spend the rest of their lives giving thanks to their heavenly Father.

Chapter Seventeen

It had been four days now since Amy had come home. That's what they were calling it, "Amy's home coming," they had told everyone the good news. In fact there was one person that Missy wanted very much to tell, so she had asked her mother, "Please Mama, I want to go tell Vicky Marie. I want to tell her that Amy got her miracle cause of our spirit warfare."

Debbie decided she needed to tell Missy she shouldn't flaunt her successes at people. "Remember we didn't know all these things either, not until we met Lil and Peter."

Missy thought it over, before she said, "I don't want to brag about it Mama, I just want to share it. Besides, I don't think Vicky Marie ever saw a miracle before, so this will help her to know that they are real."

How could Debbie argue with that, "Are you sure you're not still upset with her for going home last week?"

"No Mama, I was never upset with her. I got kind of mad at myself for letting her convince me that Missy was a baby name. I promise I will be careful with Vicky, cause I want her to get to know Jesus."

Again Debbie couldn't argue with what her daughter was saying. In so many ways Melisa seemed to understand these things better than Debbie did.

"Alright you can go talk to Vicky, but if you're going to be there any longer than an hour have her mother call me." Missy went to the curb and looked carefully, before she crossed the street. When she got to the other side she turned and waved to Debbie.

At almost exactly one hour Missy was back home. She came in through the kitchen and she sat down at the table where Debbie was working on some bills. When she didn't say anything and Debbie couldn't stand it any longer, she said, "Well. Aren't you going to tell me what happened?"

Missy grinned a somewhat mischievous grin, before she answered, "Mama when I got there I told Vicky's mom that I had to go home in one hour. I figured that way I could leave if things got too bad."

Debbie said, "Okay, good thinking. Now please go on."

"Vicky seemed happy to see me and she said she was sorry for telling me that Missy was a baby name. Then she told me that she sometimes gets tired of using two names and that I should just call her Vicky from now on. Mama, I told her about Amy waking up and how I had the dream, so I knew she was coming back way before anyone else did. And she thought that was really cool."

"And then she wanted to know if she could come with me some time to visit Amy and I said I would ask Amy's mama if that would be alright."

Debbie went over and gave Missy a hug, "Missy I am so proud of you. How did you get so smart?"

Missy hugged her mama back, and said, "I guess I must have gotten smart from you and Papa and maybe a little from Amy, cause she's really smart."

After Missy had a snack she went to play in her room for a while. Debbie decided to call David and brag a little about their daughter. She was thinking, here I am tell Missy not to brag and I'm about to do some bragging of my own. I just feel so fortunate and proud to have such a darling little girl. And so I am going to do just that.

David was also delighted to hear how his daughter had handled things with her new little friend. "We just continue to be astounded by our daughter's spiritual awareness. I hope you won't take this wrong, but Missy is sort of like a miniature Lil, in the spirit."

Debbie said, "I have to agree, and I can't think of anyone I would rather have our daughter take after spiritually, than Lil Iverson."

After David hung up from talking to Deb about their incredible daughter, he reflected about the letter he had finally sent off to Miss Hollister. He thought I'm really glad I waited to write until after the Lord brought Amy home. Surely Miss Hollister will be touched when she hears about the two little girls that came back from the heavenly garden. If anything would convince her to sell the book, surely this would be it. "Dear Lord, it is in your hands, please give us favor with Miss Hollister. Amen."

Patricia was pleased when she read the letter from David. "Dear Lord, I am sure these are the right people. Thank you Lord." Just then Melody, Miss Patricia's companion and friend came in the side door carrying some flowers from the garden.

"Hi. Is there anything worthwhile in the mail today?" She asked.

"Yes Meli, there is. In fact, I believe I have just received the answer to my prayers."

"Really," said Melody, "Whatever could that be?"

Miss Patricia poured each of them a cup of tea and said, "Please come and sit down. I would like to share this with you. Meli, you know better than anyone how long I have been looking for someone to pass my beloved copy of "The Garden of Blessings" to. Well, I want you to read this lovely letter I just received. I think you will agree that these are the people I've been waiting for."

Melody took the letter and began to read it. Then Miss Pat said, "Would you please read it out loud?"

"Yes, of course."

Dear Miss Hollister,

I have been procrastinating about this letter for some time, because I was concerned that you would turn me down. You see I am interested in buying your copy of, "The Garden of Blessings". I really would like to own this special book but I'm quite sure you must really be attached to it also. However, we have had ourselves still another miracle, so I felt the Lord prodding me to get this letter sent. So without further delay, here is our story.

Earlier this year our six year old daughter Melisa was ill with a fever and she ended up slipping into a coma. At the hospital we met the Iversons, a lovely Christian couple who also had a daughter "Amy" in a coma. Through their ministering, we came to know the Lord and we have also become the best of friends.

After much prayer, our daughter Melisa was returned to us perfectly whole. And Miss Hollister, she came back with stories of a heavenly garden and ministering angels. She also told us that she had met (seven year old) Amy in the garden. After sharing Missy's story with Lil Iverson, we discovered that the dreams Lil had about the garden, were very similar to what Missy saw. This of course blessed all of us, but it especially blessed Lil. Because she had been having dreams about being a visitor to the garden where she had actually been able to see and talk with Amy for quite some time.

Lil also talk about reading a book in the garden. The book was entitled, "The Garden of Blessings". I must admit that my search started as a lark. I had no idea that I would end up finding such a book.

But I must not get sidetracked. Having our daughter home, made all of us focus even more, on praying little Amy back home to Peter and Lil. My daughter's faith has been an amazing thing to watch, as the weeks went by she never once gave up on her little friend. My wife Debbie and I have been very blessed as we have watched the Lord move through one miracle after another. And yes, Amy came back to her mother and father last week and is making great strides in her recovery.

What more can I tell you Miss Hollister, except to say that all of us are praising the Lord Jesus for these wonderful miracles. When I spoke to Mrs. Annabelle Towns last month, she told me that you said that the Lord would let you know when the right people came along. I must say, I can't help but hope that we are (the right people). Either way, it has blessed me just knowing that the book exists. It is just another witness to the glory of God. Thank you, for your consideration Miss Hollister and may God Bless you.

Sincerely, David Miller

Melody, looked up with tears in her eyes and said, "Oh Miss Pat, you are absolutely right; it seems to me that the Lord is in this. What are you going to do?"

"I'm going to send Mr. Miller a letter and I am going to give them the book. There's no way you can sell a priceless book."

"You're right, as usual Miss Pat. I'm sure they are going to be very pleased."

"Melody, I must admit I was getting a little worried, because I've been feeling just a little bit weary lately." Then Patricia laughed and added, "Of course, I should have known, *(The Lord is always right on time)."*

In the meantime things were busy at the Iversons. Tracy had been working with Amy for quite a few days and Amy was being a real trooper about the whole routine. When Tracy walked into Amy's room that morning she found Amy already sitting on the edge of her bed. "Hey, that's a good girl. How's my favorite patient this morning?"

Amy, who still had that sense of humor that she had before the accident said, "I bet you say tha to all yur preddy paysents."

"Oh Amy, you are such a clown. I already love this job, and now are you ready for some hard work?" They were working on getting strength in Amy's legs and arms.

They had put a bar over her bed to help her pull herself up. "Okay Tracy, I reddy."

Lil walked in about an hour later, and asked, "How are things going?" Lil was surprised to see Amy already standing and attempting to use the parallel bars.

"Wow Amy, I'm so proud of you." Then she turned to Tracy and asked, "Isn't it kind of soon for her to be trying to walk?"

Tracy said, "Yes, under normal circumstances it would be. But Amy is such a trooper and besides we have some supernatural help."

Lil smiled. She could almost imagine a couple of angels, one on each side of her daughter, helping her walk again. She had already noticed that Amy's muscle tone was improving daily.

Then she said to Tracy, "I don't know why I'm so surprised. God is doing exactly what we've been praying for."

Chapter Eighteen

Lil had invited Missy and Debbie for lunch again, only this time Debbie was providing the sandwiches and chocolate cake for desert. Lil had the kitchen table all set up and Missy was tickled pink to see Amy sitting in an easy chair they had brought in to the kitchen just for her.

Debbie was truly amazed to see the progress Amy had made. "Amy sweetheart, you look great."

Amy just beamed and since Missy called Lil her auntie, Amy had taken up the idea, and thus she said, "Than you Aunt Debbee."

Missy who was also impressed with her best friends improvement piped up, "Hey and you're talking real good too."

"Yes Sunny Milsee." That got a big grin out of Missy.

As they sat at the table eating, Missy's mind was wandering back to the dream, when she had found out that Amy was coming home. Suddenly she remembered something she had totally forgotten.

She blurted out, "Oh nooo! I forgot about the baby!" Everyone was looking at Missy, who was totally embarrassed now. She was covering her mouth with both of her hands. "I'm sorry. It's just that I forgot until right now, Mama I'm so sorry." Missy left the table in tears.

Debbie got up and followed her into the living room, "It's okay Missy, but how did you know about the baby?"

Missy looked puzzled as she stared up at her mother and tried to wipe away her tears. She finally asked, "But Mama, how did you know? I found it out when I was at the fountain of blessings before Amy came home, but then I forgot to tell you."

Debbie was holding Missy now. "Missy I just found out for sure, a few days ago. Your father and I were going to tell you this evening. But it's okay that you already knew. It's just more of the blessings that have been sent to all of us."

Missy dried her tears, "I should have told you right away, but I guess I was so happy about Amy, I just forgot."

Debbie wiped a tear from her daughter's face, "I think it's very special that you already knew. Are you going to be okay now?"

Debbie had gotten up and was ready to head back to the kitchen when she realized that Missy hadn't moved. She sat back down, "Is there something else you want to tell me?" Debbie could read the signs, her daughter still sat with her head hanging down.

"Yes Mama. I know something else, but I don't know if I should tell."

Debbie wasn't quite sure what to do here. She finally said, "Missy if there is something else you know, you do need to tell me."

Missy looked up at her mama and she still had tears. And then in a tiny whisper she said, "Mama, we're going to have a baby boy."

Missy said this so softly and with such awe that Debbie hardly knew how to take it all in. After a minute or two, all she could come up with was, "Wow!" . . . .

In the kitchen Amy was grinning. So Lil asked her, "Do you know what this is all about?"

Amy was so happy that if she could have, she would have gotten up and run around the kitchen, "It real good news Momme, but I let Aunt Debee tell you."

Lil sat there wondering what was going on and thinking she wasn't sure she could handle any more surprises. She finally said, "I don't know how many more blessings we can hold, our cup is already running over."

Debbie came in and said, "I think you will be able to handle this blessing, "Auntie Lil." But Debbie was feeling so light headed she was having a hard time getting it out. She finally turned to Missy and said, "Why don't you go ahead and tell your auntie the good news."

Missy climbed up to stand on one of the kitchen chairs, and announced, "We are going to have a baby boy!"

Lil couldn't wait to tell Peter the news. She had been totally surprised, even though she was thrilled for Debbie and David. Missy was so cute and so sensitive. When she had blurted out the news of a baby Lil had no idea where this baby story was going.

Now as she prepared dinner she thought, "A person could write a whole book about all these blessings". Then she chuckled to herself as she thought of Gladys and how she had wanted one of those blessins'. It looked as if everyone in this little group had gotten at least one blessing and some even more.

Lil had given Gladys the day off because everything was going so well. Lil's heart was filled with praise as she sent a Psalm of praise to the Lord from Psalm 103:1, *"Bless the Lord, O my soul; And all that is within me, bless His holy name."* Lil got so caught up in praise; she didn't hear Peter come in until his voice joined hers in thanks to God.

Amy, who was in the recliner, clapped her hands. And then she said, "Me too."

Lil and Peter sat down with Amy, as she told her dad that they had a surprise for him, "Can I tell him Momme, since I knu before anyone else?"

Lil said, "I don't see why not."

Amy grinned at her dad, as she told him, "Missy going ta have a lil brudder."

It took Peter a minute to react to the news, he was not sure he heard Amy right, "Is she really? Lil did I hear right, are Debbie and David expecting?"

Lil nodded, and said, "They sure are and Amy knew about it while she was still in the garden. Amy told Missy about it right before she came home. And apparently Missy forgot to tell Debbie, in all the excitement of Amy's home coming."

Peter said, "Wow what a surprise this is. Does David know?"

Amy said, "Yes, he kno for two daz, but Missy feel bad."

127

Lil went on to tell Peter what had happened that afternoon. She told him how poor Missy had thought she was in trouble, because she had forgotten to tell Debbie.

Finally Peter said, "I think we're all going to need bigger houses."

Amy said, "To hold babies?"

"No." answered Peter, "To hold all these blessings." They all laughed over what Peter had said.

Everyone was quiet for a while and then Amy said, "Momme, I think mabee we need a baby too, I wood like to have a lill sisser."

Peter heard what Amy said and piped in, "Yeah Lil, what about it? It sounds like a good idea to me." Peter said this as he came up behind Lil and gave her an affectionate kiss on the cheek. "What do you say Lil? Should we start to work on a sibling for Amy?"

Lil was blushing, "Oh you two stop teasing. We just got Amy back. And I think we need to concentrate on her for a while, before we try adding to our family."

Then Lil suddenly looked at Amy and asked, "Amy, you didn't hear a baby at the fountain for us, did you?"

Amy saw her mother's near panic, "No Momme I didn't, but I bet if I did you be happee right now."

Peter gave his wife a loving look and added, "Yes Lil, I'll bet you would be just as happy as Debbie, because it's your nature." Lil knew they were right. It was just that she had been so wrapped up in Amy for the last two years. She hadn't given any thought to adding to their family. She sent a silent prayer to the Lord, (If it be your will Lord, all things are possible).

As the family settled down to bed they each had thoughts of little babies going around in their heads. Lil was thinking about tiny little pastel clothing, while Peter thought of those first building blocks and little pull toys. Amy was busy thinking of how she would be a big sister to a baby sister or brother.

Amy prayed, "Dear God, I wood be happee with either one," then Amy quickly added, "And oh yes, my Momme and Dadde are very special peopol," as she remembered the requirement of the fountain of blessings.

Peter was thrilled to hear from Dr. Gordman who had called to invite Peter to meet for lunch at the country club. He had also suggested that Peter bring David. He wanted to hear a new convert's perspective on the gospel.

Peter agreed to pick David up at the school. David was excited as he jumped into the car and said, "I managed to finagle an extra hour for lunch by making a trade with another teacher. After all, it's not every day that I get an invite to the country club. Has the good Doctor said anymore about a commitment?"

Peter looked over at David, "No he didn't say a word about that. He simply asked us to lunch. I am hopeful that a commitment is what he has in mind, but we'll just have to let the Holy Spirit lead us David."

David said, "I'm afraid I'm like a bull in a china shop when it comes to listening to the Spirit. I'll tell you one thing I could take lessons from Melisa. She is amazing."

Peter laughed and said, "Lil told me about how she handled her friend from across the street. Missy seems very sensitive in the spirit, especially for someone that's only six years old. Hey, I wanted to ask you. How do you feel about the new blessing the Lord is giving you?"

David shook his head, "Ecstatic, scared, thrilled and a bit nervous, but over all I'm doing well. I can't get over how my life has changed lately, but I'm certainly glad that it did. Debbie and I were doing fine and yet we both knew that something was missing. Now we couldn't be happier, thanks in part to you and Lil."

Peter said, "We were just messengers David and we feel fortunate to have been there at the right time."

Peter drove into the country club parking lot. "Well here we are. Let's go find out what's on Doctor Gordman's mind."

Dr. Gordman was waiting by his car as they pulled into the lot. He stepped forward and greeted Peter and David, "I'm so glad that you agreed to meet me here. I rarely take advantage of the club. I like it fine, but it's just that I don't have a lot of time."

David leaned forward to shake the doctor's hand and said, "Thanks for having us Dr. Gordman. This is quite a treat for a school teacher."

"Please, both of you just call me Joel. Today I am here as a friend in need of your friendship." They all agreed and went inside to have lunch and to become better acquainted.

Peter was pleased with Joel's easy manner. Their conversation covered a variety of subjects and yet it always came back to what Peter and David believed and why they believe it.

Finally Peter asked, "Joel have you ever read the gospel of John?"

"No, I confess I have read very little of the Bible. While I was in college there were a lot of different movements going on. There was a lot of talk about philosophy. I have no background and my parents are not spiritual at all. I think at that time, I thought religion was archaic, or at best a crutch. I'm sure you've heard that before.

"However, there was one group of kids that met early every morning. They were quiet about their faith not at all pushy. I'm sure they would have talked to me if I would have approached them. I felt a pull even then, but I talked myself out of it. I'm not going to let myself off the hook this time. Peter and David, I want the truth! Will you help me find it?"

For a minute, Peter thought David was going to get up and start running around the room. But when he saw the look that Peter gave him, he managed to settle back into his chair. Peter took a gospel of John from his pocket and handed it to Joel and said, "Why don't you start with John's gospel. Read it carefully and write down any questions you might have. And then next week we'll meet again, only next time we'll take you to lunch."

Joel walked Peter and David out to the parking lot. "I have to say the two of you project a peace and joy which I could sure use. Thanks for meeting with me. I will read the gospel and I'll give you a call."

After they had thanked their host, Peter drove David back to the school. Peter looked over at David and said, "For a minute there I thought you were going to jump up and start shouting praises or something."

David said, "I think I might have if I hadn't seen that look you gave me, I still get pretty carried away. Then when Joel came right out and stated that he wanted the truth. Well, what do you expect from a baby Christian? I'll bet you a dollar he calls before the weekend, because I recognize that hungry look."

Peter's response was, "Yeah, I thought that I had seen that look recently. But seriously David, don't forget to pray. Remember that's our part and then God does His part." All three men went back to their jobs feeling a bit lighter.

Chapter Nineteen

———◆———

Thanksgiving Day was filled with excitement. The Millers were coming over to the Iversons for turkey dinner and Gladys had promised to stop by for a piece of pie. Amy had been home for nearly two months. She was getting around quite well with the aid of a walker. Tracy had announced that Amy would be discarding that shortly.

Needless to say, the girls were enjoying Amy's new freedom. The weather was warm for late November and Amy had gotten a promise from Peter that he would help the girls get into the tree house, for at least an hour.

Lil had agreed to let them go sometime during the late morning while the dinner preparations were going on. The one stipulation was that under no circumstance was either girl to go up the ladder alone. No matter that Peter had been reinforcing the whole thing for the last week. Needless to say he was still a bit over protective of his little girl and who could blame him.

But all in all the girls had proclaimed this to be the best Thanksgiving Day ever!

Debbie had come over early to help Lil. She had also brought fruit salad and two pies. Debbie confided to Lil, "I have no idea what David has been up to, but for the last few weeks he's been to the library at least two times a week. He finally told me last night that he has a surprise for everybody and he will present it after our dinner today."

Lil said, "Hum that is curious. I wonder what it could be."

Peter who overheard, came in just then, "I tried to get it out of him but he wouldn't tell me either. By the way Debbie, did David tell you about Dr. Gordman? Lil invited him to have dinner with us today since he lives alone. But it turns out that he and his wife are trying for reconciliation, so he's having dinner with her. Apparently they have been separated for close to a year. It looks like he's taking his commitment to the Lord very seriously. I sure hope it works out for them."

Debbie answered, "I didn't know about the reconciliation. That is good news. But David did tell me that he won a bet with you for a dollar, because it seems David was right, that the doctor would call with questions before the weekend."

Just then David came through the door and added to the conversation, "You got that right. Peter really knows how to minister. In fact I've taken to calling him, (The Fisherman)."

Peter gave David a playful punch on the arm and said, "Yeah and you better cut that out. I've already told you that Lil is the spiritual one."

The two men did a little sparring back and forth, as the wives laughed at their husbands.

Then Amy hollered from the front room, "Hey Daddy. When are we going to the tree house? Remember you promised."

Lil laughed, and said, "Yeah daddy, you promised. In fact, why don't you and David go ahead and get that out of the way while Deb and I get to work on this dinner."

Amy and Missy got their coats on. Then Peter helped Amy outside and finally they all stood at the base of the big oak tree.

"See it Missy. Isn't it cool? I can't wait for us to get up there. Daddy did you put some of my books and games in the tree house, like I asked?"

Peter said, "Yes, Your Royal Princess. I did as you requested."

"Oh Daddy your being silly, but thank you for doing my bidding." Amy said this with a big grin. She was still the little clown that her father adored so much.

"Okay, let's get you two up into the club house. Who gets to go first?" Amy gave Missy the honors. So up she went with just a little help from her dad. Then Peter went up the ladder and leaned over to receive Amy from David.

"Don't you just love it Melisa? I could hardly wait to share it with you. Next summer we can start the club up again, with Jimmy, Nic, Scott and Kathleen and her little sister and brother

Marcie and Timmy. They're already members. Then there will be you and your new friend Vicky."

Missy was in absolute awe. She answered Amy, "I do love it Amy. It's very cool. Thank you so much!"

Peter climbed down and then told Amy, "Okay we will leave you on your own for one hour. David and I will be in the garage, so use the whistles if you need anything before the hour is up."

Each of the girls had a whistle on a chain in their pockets to blow in case of an emergency. "Okay Daddy, thank you." Missy was making herself right at home. They had a sleeping bag and big pillows to sit on. And true to his word, Peter had brought up some books, puzzles and games.

"Oh Amy this is so neat. I wish I had a big tree in my yard but all of our trees are still really small."

Amy gave a mischievous grin and said, "Well, I guess you'll just have to keep coming here." They both yelled, "Yea!" And then they gave each other a high-five.

Missy read a story out loud from one of the books and then they played a couple of games. They sang a few Christian songs that Missy had learned. Then Amy suddenly got serious and said, "Didn't I tell you in the garden that we were going to be best friends?"

Missy got up from her pillow and sat down by Amy and gave her a big hug and said, "Yes you did. And I told everyone that you had told me that. And that's how I knew you had to come back." The two best friends were still holding one another when Amy heard Peter say, "Hey girls it's been an hour. It's time to come down."

Both girls, surprised at how fast the hour had gone, chimed in together and said, "No way!" But Peter had already climbed the ladder to help Amy down and then Missy. The girls happily went back inside to watch a Thanksgiving Day special.

As the families sat down to Thanksgiving dinner, they were all aware of how very much they had to be thankful for. The two girls had matching dresses which Lil had made for them. The dresses were a green heather plaid, with white collars and cuffs. It seemed the perfect color for both girls.

The adults were also all decked out in their festive clothing. Peter and David took pictures. Finally Peter set up his tripod to get at least one picture showing everyone together. As he quickly joined the others they all said, "Cheese!" . . . .

Then they all joined hands and gave thanks for their families and friends. And of course they gave many thanks for two very special blessings, named Melisa and Amy. They all knew that Amy was an absolute miracle and so was Melisa. And both families knew who deserved the glory. And so with one accord they all gave thanks to God.

After the dinner and the cleanup they did a little praise and worship led by Debbie, who had brought her guitar. Everyone joined in including Gladys, who came by accompanied by Tracy and Raymond. The young couple only stayed long enough to announce their engagement and then they were off to celebrate with some friends. Gladys, however, said she was stayin for some of that pie.

After the desert everyone just sat around enjoying each other's company. They talked about how blessed and thankful they all were. Then Lil remembered David's surprise so she asked, "Okay David, you've been hinting at a surprise for quite some time now and we all want to know what it is."

Peter looked at his friend and agreed, "Yes David. What's this all about? What have you been up to?"

David stood up and said, "Okay, I'll show you. Gladys, would you please go get the girls. They will want to see this too."

Gladys brought the girls out and they sat down on the floor. And now, all eyes were on David.

David walked over to the coat closet where he had hidden the surprise. He took out a box that was wrapped in silver paper with a big white bow on the top.

David stood there for a few seconds with his head down, very much like Missy does when she's not sure what to do. Then he walked over to Lil and handed her the box before saying, "I think this has to go to you even though we will all enjoy it. You should definitely be the one to open it."

Lil took the box from David. It was not very big. It was about one foot by one foot and maybe two inches deep. Lil carefully removed the bow and then the paper. She knew without words, that this was something special.

Everyone watched as she lifted the lid. Inside all wrapped up in tissue paper was a book. As she pulled the tissue paper away the title was revealed, "The Garden of Blessings". Lil let out a little gasp, but didn't speak. Finally Amy pulled herself up onto the couch by her mother and said, "Oh Mommy, it's the book from the garden."

Lil had tears in her eyes as she looked up at David. She said, "Where in the world did you find it? And how?"

David sat down next to Debbie and began to explain how he had gotten a hold of a heavenly book. "I have to admit that at first it was just a lark. I went looking at the library and doing a little search. I wanted to see if such a book ever existed.

"Then one of the ladies at the library told me about a web site that searches out old books. So I went there and discovered to my surprise, that a book by this title was written in 1909. I kept at it until I found a copy, which was owned by an elderly lady.

I wrote her a letter telling her about our story and I asked her if she would please consider selling me the book. She sent me this letter along with the book. Then David read the letter out loud.

Dear Mr. Miller,

I received this book on my seventh birthday, Dec 2nd 1927, from my father. It was already a collector's item, as it seems there were only 100 copies printed. My father was very dear to me. He passed away when I was only ten years old, so there is no way I could ever think of selling this precious book.

However, once I read your story about the two darling little girls and their mothers. I decided to give you the book. You see, I do not have any children of my own to pass the book to. And I have felt for some time that the Lord was leading me to pass the book on. So I want you to have my precious copy of this anointed book. I hope that all of you will cherish it as much as I have.

Sincerely Yours, Miss Patricia Hollister.
P.S. Please notify me that you have received the book in good condition.

Lil just couldn't believe her eyes as she lifted the book from the box and held it up so everyone could see the cover. There was a picture of a flower garden, with flowering trees and bushes of every kind. The book was in excellent condition considering how old it was.

"David this is unbelievable. Whatever made you think there could really be such a book?"

David shrugged his shoulders, "Really, I had no idea this would happen. Truly it was just a lark at first. But then one thing led to another. Then I finally talked to this one lady that said she knew of such a book. I was stunned. She went on to say she only knew of two existing copies. I asked her a little about the book. I was still thinking it couldn't possibly be the one you read in heaven. And then she told me the clincher. She said the book she was talking about had a little girl with a pet kitten. And the author never gives us a name for the little girl; she is simply referred to as Toby's mistress. Apparently the author wanted each little girl that read the book, to become that little girl. Then the lady told me that the purpose of the book was to educate children about the different insects and creatures that live in our gardens. Once she told me that, I was bound and determined to get one of those books."

Gladys came over to look at the book, "I don't know if my heart can take it all in. Do you really think it's the same as the one you were readin' in the garden of blessins'?"

Lil turned the book around and set it in her lap. She said, "It's the same size and the cover looks about the same; I'm almost too nervous to open it, but here goes."

Lil opened the cover and read a little of the first page and then she flipped the pages to about page 20. She finally said, "This is very interesting. The two books are very similar, but this book is about an earthly garden with changing seasons. The roses in this book fade and die and are replaced by new ones, but in the heavenly book nothing dies. It's almost like this book was taken to heaven and underwent a metamorphosis's."

Missy asked, "What's a memorefus?"

Peter said, "I think it means the book got born again."

Lil laughed and said, "Yes that exactly what it seems like."

Amy piped up, "Hey that's neat. It's just like us because we got born again too. Read some of it Mommy."

Lil nodded and began. (Toby was chasing a garter snake and was just about to pounce when his mistress called, *"Be careful Toby, that's a snake and it might bite. Come over here and see the pretty Blue bird, and there's a Chickadee."*

Toby was still watching his catch slither off into the bushes and then he turned his attention to the birds. He thought, I wouldn't mind catching one of those, but my mistress won't let me. First she's afraid I'll get hurt and then she's afraid that I'll hurt something else. These humans are a strange bunch.)

Lil stopped her narration, "It's like in Ecc. 3, where there is a season for everything. There is a season for giving birth, for dying, sowing, reaping. This garden, although it is very beautiful, still operates under the law. It takes a lot of work to keep it beautiful. Where as in the heavenly garden everything operates by faith and nothing there ever dies."

Lil paused then said, "Remember Amy, when you picked the lilacs, the blooms grew right back?" Lil put the book down, and said, "David, thank you so much. We will all take turns, reading this very delightful gift. Have you notified Patricia that we received the book?"

David replied, "Yes, I sent a thank you note immediately. I find this absolutely amazing. Perhaps this book was inspired by the heavenly one."

Peter spoke up, "I think we should write a special thanks to Miss Patricia. I just realized that she will be 89 years old this Dec. 2nd."

Debbie added, "That's a great idea Peter and maybe you girls would like to make a nice card or a picture to put in with our letter."

Both girls were ready to get started. Amy said, "Didn't I tell you that this would be the best Thanksgiving Day ever!"

Chapter Twenty

The girls were busy making their drawings so they could be added to the letter. They both wanted to send Miss Patricia a picture of the heavenly garden. Amy was doing a lilac bush with an angel standing by it, and Missy was drawing the fountain. Missy said, "Maybe when she sees our drawings she won't be afraid to go there, cause she'll know how nice it is."

The girls were almost through when Missy looked up from her drawing and asked her mama, "Why didn't they send a baby from the fountain to Miss Patricia? I'll bet she would have really liked that, cause she must have been kind of lonely." Debbie hesitated, wondering where these insights came from.

Then Amy piped up and said, "Only God can make those decisions. I'm praying for a sister or a brother, but Mommy says that it is in God's hands. I sure hope he decides in my favor."

Debbie was writing the letter to Miss Patricia, telling her how grateful they were that she had sent the book to them. All of a sudden Amy practically shouted, "I have a great idea! Why don't we send Miss Patricia one of the heavenly lilac's we pressed?"

Lil, who was sitting there listening and was still in awe at the heavenly book agreed. "That's a wonderful idea Amy. I'll go find something sturdy to ship them in."

Once they had put everything together Debbie sat down and read the letter she had written to Miss Patricia out loud.

Dear Miss Hollister,
We do not have adequate words to properly thank you for your precious gift. We do want to assure you that we will take every precaution to keep your book in as good a condition as possible.

We are grateful that the story of our two little girls touched your heart. And they are very insistent that I tell you a little about the heavenly garden that they both experienced. Amy said to tell you that an angel told her there are many gardens in heaven and they are all very beautiful.

Missy wants for you not to be afraid to go to heaven, because Jesus will meet you there and show you everything!

Lil Iverson is Amy's mother, and she was a visitor to the heavenly Garden of Blessings. She asked me to tell you of the incredible peace she always felt while she was there.

We have also included some pressed lilacs that Lil was allowed to bring back with her from the Heavenly Garden. This is all very supernatural, but I have a feeling that you already understand the miraculous.

All of us will enjoy your very special book and even the men had tears in their eyes when they saw your gift. With much appreciation, we send our love and prayers.

In His name, The Millers and the Iversons

They all prayed over the package after it was all put together. David would take it to the post office the next day . . . .

The following week when Patricia got her mail she was surprised to see the heavy cardboard envelope. She took her mail to her little sun room and sat down to open the package.

"Dear Lord, what is all this?" She said, as she looked at the things in the envelope. She smiled as she admired the drawings. And she especially liked the lilacs from heaven.

"Oh my, aren't these lovely." she said. And then she read the letter written by Debbie and she felt very sure that she had passed the book on to the right people. She started to get up from her chair, when a small piece of blue paper fell away from the others. She picked it up and unfolded it. Then she began to read the tiny print.

Dear Miss Pat, I wanted to thank you for the book. I will pray for you every day. I am so sad that they did not give you a baby from the fountain of blessings. But I believe that you have a special blessing waiting for you in heaven so you will never be lonely again. I love you Miss Pat. Missy . . . . (Dear Patricia I helped Missy write this, so it would be legible. She is a very spiritual child, and she insisted on the part about the baby from the fountain of blessings. I hope you are not offended. Thank you, Miss Patricia, from the bottom of my heart.) Lil Iverson

As Patricia read the tiny note from Missy, she felt her heart both soar and fall as she thought to herself. How did Missy know? Out loud she prayed, "God bless your sweet little messenger."

Pat felt tired as she picked up the lilacs that Lil had somehow fastened to cardboard and then covered in a hard clear plastic. She thought, "This would be nice put in a frame. Perhaps I can ask Melody to do that for my birthday . . . . It's only three days off. I can hardly believe I will be eighty nine years old. All these years, how did Missy know how lonely I've been? She must be a very sensitive child."

Patricia went over and sat down on the sofa. She sunk down into its soft cushions. "I'll just lay back and rest for a while, until Melody gets home to fix my supper. Thank you, dear Lord for Meli. And thank you for those precious little girls that you sent back to their families."

It had been about an hour when Melody came in with the things that she had bought to fix Miss Pat's dinner. She thought it seemed awfully quiet.

She put down her bags and walked into the living room, as she called out, "Miss Patricia dear, are you out here in the sun room? It's a perfect day for sitting out here." Melody stopped as she entered the sun room, when she saw Miss Pat lying on the sofa. Miss Pat never took a nap, she always said, (naps were a waste of one's valuable time).

Melody already knew as she knelt down to check her dear friend that she was no longer with us. Melody still felt for a pulse even though she knew, "Dear Lord, I know that she is with you now."

As Melody rose from the floor she saw that Miss Pat was holding something in her arms. She gently pulled the cardboard with the lilacs, the letter and the drawings from her friend's arms. Then she saw the little blue note, clutched in Miss Pat's hand. She set them on the table. Then she went to call Dr. Morris. He was a dear friend to both of the women and he would know what needed to be done . . . .

The funeral was held the day before Patricia's, eighty ninth birthday. There were only a few people from their little church. Pat had always said, (It's not good to outlive all of your friends and most of my friends are already in heaven.)

Melody was thinking about the great reunions taking place in heaven for Miss Pat. What a special lady she was. There were also quite a few women at the funeral. This did not surprise Melody, as she thought, (There would have been a lot more, if there had been more time for people to make the trip.)

When she got home from the funeral Melody felt a little lost as she began straightening things up. Melody read the letter and the little note from Missy. Her friend had made a good choice sending the book to these people.

She stopped what she was doing and once again thanked the Lord for her very dear friend. Tears filled her eyes as her thoughts drifted back and she began to reflect on the day she had met Miss Pat.

Part Two
Patricia Hollister and Melody Harris

Chapter Twenty One

———————◆———————

Melody had been in trouble, she was pregnant and she was only seventeen. Her father had kicked her out of the house, and he had told her, (Don't cha ever come back here, agin. Do ya hear me?)

She had heard alright, she had gone to her friends, but they told her their parents wouldn't let them help. Terri her best friend, had given her 20 dollars. And then there was the boy, the one who had said he loved her. Well, he had taken off with some friends to make it big in California. He said he'd be back, but she knew that she would never see him again.

Melody was so tired and hungry, that she had finally gone to a soup kitchen. At least there she could get something to eat. She had decided that she wanted to keep the baby, but she had no idea how she would handle it. She needed a job.

She sat down with her soup at a table, "Oh God, what am I going to do? Please tell me what to do." It was then as she looked up through her tears, that she saw Miss Patricia for the first time. She had come over and sat down across from Melody. She had brought her a piece of bread to go with her soup. "Here you are dear; this will help to fill the empty spots."

She took the bread and ate it with the soup. She didn't want to leave. It was nice and warm here and she had nowhere to go. As the tables began to fill up, she knew she needed to move on.

Melody got up and left the warm building. Again she cried out, "God I don't know what to do, I am so afraid." . . . . She could no longer hold back the tears that came in a deluge, as she sunk to the ground just outside of the door.

She was sobbing so hard that her body shook and then she felt hands pulling her to her feet. And there was the kind *voice telling her. "Everything is going to be alright dear." It was Miss Pat and she had pulled her to her feet and put a blanket around her shoulders.*

Then she had put Melody in her car and had taken her to her little home. Miss Pat had taken her in and provided food and a place to sleep. She told Melody that she needed help with the cleaning and cooking, so Meli (her new nick name) would have to earn her keep.

It didn't take long to figure out that Miss Pat really didn't need any help. But she never once made Meli feel like she was taking a hand out. She made her feel wanted for the first time since her mother had died. Melody had only been twelve years old at the time and her mother had provided the only stability that she had ever known. Her father lived in the bottle and he didn't need another mouth to feed.

She had managed to stay out of his way, until she got pregnant. She knew it was wrong from the beginning. Her mother had taken her to church and taught her what was right. But she had been so lonely; she just wanted to be loved.

Now, she was learning what true love was all about. This kind woman had introduced her to Jesus and she told her that Jesus would never leave her, nor forsake her.

Melody had explained to Miss Pat, that the reason she was named Melody, was because her mother said, "The day that you were born, God put a song in my heart." Meli had begun to believe that someday she would be reunited with her mother. Because now she knew, there really was a heaven.

Melody felt sure that Miss Patricia had saved her life the night she took her in. And even though she had lost the baby after just a few weeks, Miss Pat had told her she wanted her to stay. She had said, "I've become somewhat attached and I hope you are comfortable here dear."

Of course the answer had been, "Yes Miss Pat, I am very comfortable."

Thus the years had passed. Melody had gone to nursing school and gotten her degree. She had worked in order to go to school, but there is no mistaking the fact that Miss Patricia had become her mentor. She was also her best friend and the grandmother she'd never had. Meli had become Miss Pat's companion and friend and then toward the end, she had become her nurse.

The Millers had gotten a phone call from Melody Harris to inform them that Patricia had passed away, just three days before she would have turned eighty nine years old.

Melody told them that yes, Pat had received the things they had sent. She told Debbie, "Miss Pat, that's what I always called her. Well, when I found her she had the things you had sent pressed to her bosom and the little blue note was clutched in her hand next to her heart."

Debbie asked, "What blue note?" and then when Melody read it to her, she knew of course that Missy had added it to the other things.

Melody went on to say, "I believed that Missy's little note touched my friend very deeply. I am sending you all a letter, in which I will try to introduce you to and also explain to you a very complicated woman. Miss Pat was a true lady that took care of me through my darkest hour.

"I think once you read my account of this truly remarkable woman's story, then you will understand better why she wanted you to have the book and also why little Missy's note struck a chord in her heart."

Debbie said, goodbye to Melody and she had also extended an invitation to Melody to please come and visit. Debbie made a call to Lil and Peter, She told Lil, "I'm afraid I have some sad news. Miss Patricia has gone home to be with the Lord. Why don't you bring Amy over here and we will tell the girls together." They decided on about eleven o'clock . . . .

When Lil and Amy arrived, Debbie had set out a light lunch. She had figured that no one would have much of an appetite once they heard the news of the death of their benefactor.

After letting the girls know that Miss Patricia was in heaven, Debbie held her daughter on her lap. Poor little Missy started sobbing; "I knew Miss Patricia was lonely for someone who had already gone to heaven."

Amy said, "Oh, you mean her father that she lost just three years after he gave her the book."

"No," Missy said, "There was someone else . . . ."

Debbie looked over at Lil. And then she asked Missy, "How did you know sweetheart? Did someone in heaven tell you?"

"No, I just knew. I guess the same way I knew what Amy wanted."

Amy who also had tears streaming done her cheeks; spoke up, "I think she knew it in her spirit."

Both Lil and Debbie sat there a little stunned by their daughter's spiritual awareness. Lil finally said, "We are all very sad for ourselves, but I think we should be happy for Miss Pat, because now she's with the people she lost."

The girls agreed that Miss Pat was now with the people she loved. So they dried their tears and headed for Missy's room to watch a video that Debbie had bought about angels.

Debbie went on to tell Lil more about Melody and she thanked Lil for helping Missy write the note. And then she told Lil about the letter that was on its way from Melody.

After Lil and Amy had gone on home Missy told her mother, "Mama when I wrote the note to Miss Patricia, I just knew there was someone in heaven that she wanted to see again. Do you really think that she is with that person now?"

"Yes darling I do, I believe the people we love, who have gone on to heaven will also be there to greet us when it's our time to go."

Missy frowned, "But Mama, I didn't see Grand Ma when I was in the garden?"

Debbie shook her head as she considered what Missy said, "I think that you and Amy were in a special garden, perhaps one that's just for children that are sick or that are in comas. I don't really know for sure, but I do believe it was different from the heaven we will go to when we die. The

148

important thing is that God took care of you and Amy, just like He's taking care of all those other children. We are so blessed that Jesus loves us."

Missy nodded, "Yes, and we love Him too."

Chapter Twenty Two

Dear Friends, I would like to introduce you to _Patricia Hollister_. I feel that it is important that I write this letter to you and tell you about one of the most generous and gracious women I have ever met. Patricia was a beautiful woman both outwardly and inwardly. She was very elegant and had a regal bearing about her that demanded respect from all who met her. And yet once you got to know her, you knew that she would literally give you the shirt off of her back.

Miss Patricia Hollister took me in at a time when I had no one to turn to. She has done similar good deeds for countless young women who were left alone and desperate. I am sorry to say, I do not have the names of these women, whom I am sure would be willing to give their own glowing accounts of their experiences with Miss Hollister.

You see Miss Pat, as I will call her for the rest of this correspondence, founded and financed a foundation simply named, "Out of Step." The foundation was established to help young women who found themselves (out of step) with society.

She started this foundation at first on a small scale, furnishing a couple of small houses for the girls to live in until their delivery date. She and other women from her church provided counseling. Some of the girls kept their babies, while others gave theirs up for adoption.

Eventually the foundation grew into a home that housed as many as thirty to forty women full time. These women were loved and cared for spirit, soul and body. They were given help in finding employment and even learning skills they could use once they moved on.

I'm not quite sure how I became the lucky one that ended up being Miss Pat's companion, but I am very thankful that I did. Miss Pat was already forty five years old when I met her . . . . I just now realized that I knew her for almost half of her life. Since I was only seventeen when I met her, well you can do the math, I am now sixty one.

I became a registered nurse with the help of Miss Pat. I will fill you in on my situation at another time. Right now I want to tell you what happened in my dear friend's life, to send her on this path of aiding young unwed mothers . . . .

Patricia, as you already know, lost her father when she was only ten years old. By all accounts he was a wonderful man and generous to a fault. He simply loved helping people and since he was a banker he did just that, not only through his job, but in other ways as well.

Apparently things went well for the Hollisters, at least for the first ten years of Pat's life. Then in nineteen thirty Mr. William Hollister, became ill with pneumonia and the bank was taken over by his partner, a descent young man, but inexperienced. Without Williams' guidance, he soon made some poor investments and the bank began to fail. This happened at a time when things were already tight.

It was not long before Mr. Hollister died of complications from the pneumonia. Pat's mother had never worked and she was a rather spoiled young woman that had been pampered first by her father and then by William. She was just too immature to provide a good home for Pat. William had left a trust to Patricia that she was to receive when she was twenty four.

In the meantime Pat was knocked about from pillar to post, so to speak. Staying for a while with an elderly aunt and then with her uncle, neither had a clue what this young girl needed. Finally at eighteen, Pat was able to go out on her own.

And then in nineteen forty Pat managed to enroll in a business college. It was there that she met the love of her life, Thomas Masterson. He was a fine young man that was also studying business. His dream was to someday be a merchant, with his own store that dealt in fine silks, wools and other materials from all over the world.

He would tell Pat that when she became his wife, she would be the best dress woman in town. It had been love at first sight for both of them; they studied together and went to church together. They would take long walks and talk about their future. Pat told Tom that she wanted to work in his business. It only made sense after all; she was going to school to learn business. She told him that she would be a great help to him.

He would protests that be wanted a wife that would be there when he came home after a hard day at work. And he wanted a wife that would fix him a nice meal and have his children. Pat would laugh and simply say "I can do both". Usually Tom would concede and say I want whatever makes you happy, Patricia.

During the first year things were really grand for the young couple. It was during nineteen forty one, with news of the War in every newspaper, that the couple became concerned. Their plan was for Tom to finish up his schooling in forty two. And then he would get a good job and they would be married in June of forty three.

However, all their plans were changed on Dec. 7, 1941 when Pearl Harbor was attacked. Young men all over the country were signing up. Patricia knew that Thomas would feel that he needed to do his share. And sure enough by the first of February, Thomas had made *his* decision, he would join the Navy. As the sun set one February evening during Tom's training, Pat's heart was breaking. She knew Tom had to go, but she also knew that her life would be lived in a sort of limbo until he could return to her. On one of those lonely nights she had written these words, in her journal.

"My dearest Tom, My heart aches. Knowing that in a few days you must leave me here, to go and do what you must for your Country. Tom darling, I will never say goodbye. I will only say later. I will see you later. Until then, my heart will simply wait. Darling, I will keep you in my heart and in my prayers always." Patricia

And time had gone way too quickly for Tom and Pat. It had been hard enough when Tom had gone for his training, but Pat had been there to send him off.

Tom told her, "I am pretty sure I will get one leave before I get my orders. I will let you know by phone if I can, if not then you will get a letter. I absolutely believe we will be given at least one more day together, before I have to go. You have my heart for always Patricia."

Pat nodded through her tears, "And you have mine." Then she put her hand on her heart and said, "Tom, I'll keep you right here in my heart, no matter where you are." She waited a second then added, "I can come meet you if you can't come home on leave." As the train pulled out she shouted, "Later, I'll see you later!" . . . .

It turned out that Tom was right and he got the one leave, before getting his final orders. The couple spent as much time as possible together. They made vows and promises and I believe that Pat kept every one of those vows to Tom. There was never another man in Pat's life, not one that could fill the place she had carved out, just for her Tom.

Again the time went by much too fast, and once more Tom's train was pulling away from the station. Tom had caught on and he called out, "Later darling, I'll see you later." . . . .

It had been about six weeks before Pat knew for sure, that she was going to have Tom's child. Things had gotten

tough; she had dropped out of school and was working all the hours she could get at the local diner. It was hard work being on her feet all day.

She wrote Tom almost every day, but only got two letters from him and they were weeks old. She wondered if he had gotten the letter that would tell him he was going to be a father. "Oh God forgive me, it's just that we had so little time. Please look after Tom, bring him home safely to us."

It was the middle of May when the school telephoned Pat and asked her if she would please stop by. Pat was curious as to why they had called her, but she hurried over to the school after her shift finished on Friday the 15th.

She headed for the Dean's office, but his secretary met her in the hall. Pat knew as soon as she saw the woman's face that it was bad. "No," she said, "No, not Tom, please not Tom."

The Dean hurried out of his office and put his arm around Pat, but she was inconsolable. They took her to the school nurse who gave Pat a tranquilizer.

When she woke, she learned that Tom had died on the USS Yorktown, at the battle of the Coral Sea on May 8TH 1942. The battle had lasted for only four days (May 4-8). However the battle for Pat's life and that of her baby's had only just began.

It was already June. Tom had been dead for a whole month, but to Pat it didn't matter. She was all alone again. Tom had filled her life and for the first time since her father had died, she had had someone to love. Now he was gone and nothing would ever be the same.

Her friends tried to console her, but she had put up a wall. She asked them please, to just leave her alone. She would say things like, "I don't want to live. I can't live without Thomas. Oh God, just take me home!"

Pat wasn't eating right and she felt sick most of the time. The doctor told her she needed to take care of herself for the baby's sake. Pat couldn't hear any of them, she was just so depressed.

Then in the second week of June, Pat had finished her shift at the diner. She had finally gone back to work simply because it helped to fill the lonely hours. When she got home Sandy, one of the girls who had taken her in when she had been at her lowest, handed her a letter. It was from Tom. It was post marked May 1, 1942. Pat sunk to her knees, "Oh dear God, my Tom, it's from my Tom."

Sandy helped Pat to her bed and got her some water. And then she left Pat alone. Pat sat there for a long time before she finally got the courage to open the letter. The tears flowed freely, as she read . . . .

My Dearest Patricia,

I finally received your letter dated April 14. I can't begin to tell you how happy I am to hear about our baby. In fact, my darling, I am over the moon.

Patricia, I don't have much time now. I will write you some more when I can. But right now I want you to know for sure, I already love that baby with my whole heart.

Pat, you must take care of yourself and our precious baby. I love you both forever. Later sweetheart, I'll see you later.

Always yours, Tom

Pat sat on her bed for a long time. Tom had known about the baby before he died. The tears began to flow all over again as Pat realized what she had been doing. She had put Tom's baby in jeopardy. "Dear Lord, forgive me and please help me to go on living for Tom and for our baby."

From that day forward, Pat took the best care of herself that she could. She still had to work the long hours on her feet but she ate right and slept when she could . . . .

For some reason, Pat had developed a sort of a following after she came out of her depression. Other young women she knew seemed to feel that she must have some kind of special strength. She did have the Lord of course, but she hadn't let Him help her when she had needed Him the most.

For whatever reasons the other girls would come to her for prayer and sometimes for advice. She felt like a phony, because all she really did was pray with them and listen. The days went past slowly, as Pat grew bigger.

"Oh Lord, it is so hard. Please help me to keep going." She was in her eighth month and she didn't feel good, but she had to keep working. She had to help with the rent and food. It was hard on everyone and she was determined to do her fair share.

On November 15, Pat had gone into labor; her due date wasn't until December 9th. She had been at work when the pain started and her boss drove her to the hospital.

The labor had been long and hard but Pat gave birth to a tiny baby boy; he weighed only five pounds, but the doctor was hopeful. Pat had the name all picked out, William Thomas, after her father and after Tom. She would have put down Thomas first, but Tom had once told her, "If we ever have a boy I don't want my son being called Junior."

So it was that little William Thomas Masterson had been born on November 15, 1942. When the doctor put him into Pat's arms she had been in total awe. She said, "Oh Tom he is just so perfect. I so wish you could see him."

A nurse said, "Maybe he can, maybe he's looking down from heaven right now." Pat liked that idea, as she looked over her tiny son, counting his little fingers and toes.

"Tom you should see his dear little mouth. He's so perfect, just perfect, but I already told you that."

Pat held him as often as she could and if only love would have been enough, little William had plenty of that. The doctor said his little heart just wasn't strong enough. Little William had only lived for three days.

He had been too small the doctor said, plus they didn't have the right equipment to care for him properly. And then there was this dreadful war.

Sandy was there for Pat, but it seemed for a while that she would go back into her depression. Then Pat got out of bed on the nineteenth, to attend the funeral for little William. She would stand tall for hers and Tom's son, at least for today . . . .

That afternoon she had gone back to the little grave. She had sat and talked to Tom and to Willy who was buried next to his father. She read Tom's letter to little Willy. And she told him, "Someday when I get to heaven, I will show you just how much I love you." . . . .

Then she said, "Tom, I did the best I could for our little boy, now it's got to be up to you. I'm so glad he's not alone." When she got up to leave she turned back, and said, "Later, I'll see you both later. And remember, I love you both with all of my heart."

Patricia was aware that almost everyone had expected her to go to pieces again. But Pat had come to realize that even though it was Tom's letter that had finally woke her up, her real strength had come when she had turned back to God.

She had done what she knew her heavenly Father would have expected her to do. She had read and trusted in, *2 Cor. 1:3,4 (The God of all comfort, who comforts us in all our tribulation, so that we may be able to comfort them which are in any trouble, by the same comfort, with which we ourselves are comforted by God.)*

Now she understood why all those girls had come to her, they wanted that comfort; they had recognized the comfort that only God can give. Pat had also drawn strength from something her father had told her right before he had died.

He had said, *"Patricia, if you're trying to make a decision and you're not sure what to do, just imagine what choice you would make if God had his hand on your shoulder."* Her father had added, *"If you follow that simple rule, I think most of your choices will be good ones."*

Pat had forgotten all of that when she had lost Tom. She had not listened to her friends. She had silenced the voice of her father and she had blamed God.

When Pat thought of little William, she knew she could find a lot of places to put the blame. For one, she could blame herself because she hadn't taken care of herself at first. But she also knew that all of that anger and blame wouldn't bring her baby back and it wouldn't bring Tom back either.

So Pat had made the decision, (with the Lord's help) that for the rest of her life she would do her best to focus her energy on helping others that found themselves in hard places. It had started out with her just listening when someone needed a friend. When she could she gave money, sometimes she would take up a collection.

Little by little she got on her feet and then in December of 1944, Patricia Hollister received the trust from her father. She had known it was there, it just never occurred to her that it would end up being valued in the hundreds of thousands of dollars. That kind of money in the forties would go a very long way.

It was then that Pat had gotten serious about housing for her, "Out of Step" program. At first she rented a few homes and then she decided with the Lords help, (you know, the hand on the shoulder thing) that it would be more cost efficient if she bought some houses. Finally she remodeled an old forty room mansion and for the next forty years, she owned and operated the "Out of Step", foundation. It was a program that would help countless of young women get through some really tough times and then to go on with their lives.

I suppose I could fill a book with the stores, but I think you get the idea, so I will close now. Please enjoy the book. That's what Patricia wanted. Sincerely, Melody Harris

P.S. Perhaps someday I will come and meet you all. Thank you for the invitation.

Chapter Twenty Three

When the mail came for the Millers, they brought it to the door, because the envelope from Melody Harris was large and the mail carrier didn't want to bend it. Missy, who opened the door, was beside herself with excitement, wanting to know what was inside.

Debbie did open the envelope, but she said to Missy, "We need to wait until everyone is here, so we can all read it together." Missy was impressed with how many pages there were.

"Mama, there must be at least twenty pages."

Debbie said, "It looks like about eight to ten pages, but that is a long letter. I'm curious to see what it says too." Missy looked at the written pages trying to see if she could read any of it, but she couldn't.

Missy asked, "Can you give me a hint what it's about?"

Debbie said, "I can tell you that it's about Miss Patricia and it tells us something about her life, so we can get to know her a little bit."

"When will everyone be here? Mama, I can hardly wait." Debbie reached over and began to tickle Missy, who squealed and laughed with her mother.

When the two families were together, Lil asked Debbie if she thought there was anything in the story that Melody had sent that might upset the girls.

Debbie said, "I did go ahead and read the letter just to make sure that it was appropriate for the girls to hear. Patricia definitely experience loss in her life, but I think the girls have already figured that out. I do think that what Melody wrote will help them understand what they've already sensed."

Lil considered what Debbie said, and then she agreed, "I guess you're right; what they imagine is probably worse than the truth."

Then Debbie put her hand on Lil's arm, "Lil, remember the note you helped Missy to write?" Lil was nodding. "Well, I think I should tell you right up front. There was a baby. I believe that fact will both please and upset Missy, but I think over all it will be a blessing to both girls."

Lil whispered, "Oh my, I can't help but wonder what happened."

When everyone had settled down to hear what Melody had to say about Miss Pat. Debbie began to read.

It didn't take long before the girls wanted to know what a foundation was, so Debbie explained that it was sort of a company set up to help people. Then she told them the name, "Out of Step."

Peter said, "What a good idea and very apropos."

Missy wanted to know, "But why did they call it that?"

Lil was the one to respond, "Sometimes we just aren't ready for things that happen in our lives. Sometimes it's the right thing, but maybe it's the wrong time. The foundation helped those people out."

That seemed to satisfy the girls and so Debbie read on. She read how Miss Pat's father had died when she was only ten and how she didn't really have a good home after she lost her father.

Amy said, "That was the first person that she lost." Lil pulled Amy closer. Debbie went on to read about how Pat went to college and that it was there, she met Thomas and fell in love.

She read about the good times that they had together before Thomas had to go to war. And then how they had to say goodbye to each other. Amy spoke up and said, "But they didn't say goodbye, they always said, that they would see each other later. I think that's romantic."

This comment brought to Lil's mind, when in her dream, Amy had said that it was romantic that Peter would bring Lil a single rose; it also brought a few tears.

Missy asked, "Why did he have to go to war, Papa?"

David knew it would be hard for the girls to understand about war, but he answered, "It's because there are some bad people in the world and sometimes the good people have to fight, in order to stop them."

Missy thought on this, and then she asked, "Kind of like spirit warfare?" David nodded, "Yeah, kind of like spirit warfare. Only this kind of war is fought with regular weapons, but it's still the devil that causes it."

Debbie knew the next part would be kind of hard, so she said, "This next part of the story is going to be sad. Are you girls sure you want to hear it?"

The girls looked at each other and finally Amy said, "We want to know the truth, and sometimes the truth can be sad."

Both sets of parents sat in wonder at their little girls. They just seemed so grown up; perhaps it was because they had been to the garden.

Missy was also in agreement, they were ready for the truth. But she did add, "I still might cry, even if I want to know the truth."

So Debbie went on to read some more of the story about how Thomas had died in the war and how Pat had been so sick over the loss. By now both girls were crying and so were Lil and Debbie. It took Debbie a few minutes to gain control, before she read the part about the baby.

She read how Pat gave birth and then how she had lost her little son (William). Missy was crying but she managed to say, "Mama, Miss Pat did get a baby from the fountain of blessings, she did and I'm so sorry she lost him. But now I know why she was so lonely."

Missy and Amy were both crying and hugging, but they both said, "She's with all of them now, right? She with Thomas and her baby, isn't she?"

Debbie and Lil were both crying right along with the girls, as Lil said, "Yes, they are all together and don't forget about Pat's father. I believe he is there too, with his little grandson."

By now, everyone was laughing and crying. Debbie took a little break before she finished reading the rest of Patricia story. When she finished, they all had to agree that Miss Pat was a remarkable woman. And though they hadn't ever met her in person, they still felt like they knew her.

Amy was quick to point out that, "Someday we will all meet her in heaven. And I'm so glad that Melody told us about her."

Missy added, "We'll get to meet them all, even little Willy."

Lil nodded, but she couldn't help but wonder whether William might be all grown up by then. Only God knew the answer to that question. For right now, she just felt a whole lot of joy for Patricia.

Before the Iversons and the Millers knew it, Christmas had come and gone. If the girls thought that Thanksgiving of 2009 had been the very best, Christmas was even better. Of course, the families had spent the holidays together.

Gladys had given each girl a pretty angel pin. Tracy had given them some cool board games. Their parents had a real hard time keeping the spending in line but they had accomplished this by suggesting that they send some money to Patricia's foundation. The girls had each offered to empty their piggy banks, but their moms had said that wasn't necessary. But they couldn't help feeling that they had the greatest kids ever?"

Chapter Twenty Four

The New Year brought some more surprises for the Iversons and the Millers.

Amy was improving every day and even though she was a year older than Missy, she had lost almost two years to the coma. So Lil and Deb had decided to take turns home schooling both the girls for the first grade. Needless to say, the girls thought their mothers were brilliant for coming up with such a great plan.

Lil had been working with Amy so she could catch up and it looked like the girls were going to finish out their first year of school with very high marks. Debbie's baby was due on May 27TH. And she was a little concerned that she might not be able to finish her part of the commitment if the baby should come early. Lil had told her, "You needn't worry about a thing. I'm sure I can finish out the year with the girls if the baby comes early."

The girls, who were listening to their moms, both said at once, "We can hardly wait for the baby to come."

Then they both giggled and Amy said, "Are we going to get to baby sit?"

Debbie started getting emotional, "I can't believe I'm going to be a mom again. Did I tell you that David wants to name him Peter after his best friend?"

Lil was pleased to hear this even though she had already heard it from Peter. David had already told Peter that it was what he wanted. The two men had become close friends and so had Lil and Deb. So the girls weren't the only ones to become "Best Friends." . . . .

One day at the end of March, after Debbie and Missy had left for the day and Amy had gone with them for a sleep over,

Lil had gotten the book out again. It had been a while since she had read it. She was thinking that things were finally settling down again. No more surprises.

Lil had made a special cotton quilted envelope to keep the book in and she had also covered it with a cotton quilted sleeve. They were keeping their promise to take good care of the special gift.

She had just opened the book when the telephone rang. She picked it up and said, "Hello, this is Lil."

On the other end of the line came an unfamiliar female voice which quickly identified herself as Melody Harris. Melody asked Lil if she could come by the house the next morning.

"I am just finishing up my vacation and I decided to take a chance and see if I could come by tomorrow at around ten o'clock. You see Lil; I have something that you should have, something that belonged to Miss Pat."

Lil was very curious but decided not to ask what it was that Melody had. She said, "Yes of course, please do come. I am looking forward to meeting you. And yes, ten o'clock would be fine." . . . . Well, Lil mused, perhaps there was just one more surprise.

Lil could hardly wait for Peter to come home that night, because she had a couple of surprises for him . . . .

When Peter came in the back door at six o'clock, he was surprised to see the dining room all set out with the good china and silver ware. Lil was lighting some candles and she looked absolutely beautiful in a lovely lavender dress. She smiled when Peter came in with a question written all over his face.

He said, "What's this? Did I forget an anniversary or something? And how come only two places are set? . . . . By the way Lil, you look gorgeous. I just want to know if I'm in trouble."

Lil finished lighting the candles, "No Peter, you're not in trouble, I just have a couple of really neat things to tell you and Amy is spending the night with Missy. So it's just the two of us. And since we don't get that many opportunities, I thought we would make it a romantic evening. Would that be all right with you?"

Peter felt like he was on a first date or something. He suddenly felt self-conscious and awkward. Lil could always do that to him. He went over and put on a nice romantic CD. And then he said, "If I would have known I would have brought you a single rose. I believe Amy said that was real romantic."

Lil pulled out his chair and said, "You're doing just fine." Lil had prepared a lovely dinner with steaks and baked potatoes; everything was cooked to perfection.

As Peter took the last bit; he looked up from his plate and said, "Wow Lil, the dinner was delicious but I have to admit that I 'm getting really curious."

Finally Lil said, "Would you care to guess what the surprise is?"

Peter wasn't sure where this was going, but he would give it a try. "I know you wanted that upstairs addition to your shop. Is that it?"

Lil shook her head, "No it's a little more personal than that, but go ahead and try again."

Peter had no idea, so he asked, "Has this anything to do with Amy and her progress?"

Lil thought for a second and then she said, "Okay I'm not being fair here. You could never guess the first surprise, because it was a total surprise even to me. I got a call from Melody Harris today and she wants to come by tomorrow morning. She says that she has something that belonged to Miss Pat and she thinks I should have whatever it is."

Peter raised his eye brows, "That is interesting. I take it she didn't tell you what it is."

"That's right. I must say she sure has me wondering, but for some reason I didn't feel I should ask. So I will just have to wait and see."

Peter was also wondering, "I hope you'll call me when you find out what it is. I wonder what it could be." They sat there for a while both trying to come up with an idea.

Lil said, "It could be anything. Perhaps it's another book or maybe even a piece of jewelry, it certainly is curious."

A little later as they were clearing the table, Peter remembered that Lil had said she had a couple of things to tell him. "Wait a minute; you said you had a couple of things to tell me. What's the other surprise?"

Lil put down the dishes she had, and then she took the ones Peter was holding and set them back on the table. Lil took his hand, "Come with me to the front room, I have something to show you."

When they got to the front room, Lil went over to a long narrow table, and opened the small drawer. She took out a small package wrapped in tissue, which she handed to Peter. "I think you will remember these from a few years back."

Peter took the package and carefully un-wrapped the tissue from around a tiny pair of white booties. When Peter looked up at Lil, she was sure she saw tears. Then he said, "Lil, these are the wishing booties you made about four years ago. Does this mean what I think?"

Lil was beaming now, as she nodded and said, "Yes Peter, we're going to be adding to our family. You and Amy convinced me that it was a good idea and so I prayed. This is Gods answer."

Peter was holding Lil and the booties, as he began to whirl Lil around the living room. He was shouting praises to the Lord.

Lil said, "I take it, that you're happy with the news."

"Lil you know I am. This is really wonderful. Have you told Amy?"

Lil shook her head, "I figured, that we would tell her together."

Peter was still dancing around the living room, when he said, "She will be more than just happy, she'll probably want to take full credit. You do know she's been praying for this, ever since we've known about Debbie."

Lil answered, "Yes, I know. We will tell her tomorrow and who knows, it probably was her prayers that God answered."

Lil and Peter had a lovely evening together. Amy would have said it was very romantic. Peter was still waltzing around the kitchen the next morning. He had told Lil over and over how pleased he was with the news of the baby.

Lil had asked him if he wanted a boy. He had answered, "Lil, I honestly don't care Amy loves watching football and baseball with me, so what more could I ask. Besides, I am so filled with thankfulness for just having Amy back. I figure the Lord knows best."

As if on cue, at that very moment the phone rang and it was Amy calling from Debbie's. "Hi Daddy I just wanted to call before you went to work to say I love you and to tell you goodbye."

"Thank you Amy, that is very thoughtful. I missed all that time when you couldn't tell me goodbye."

Amy said, "But Daddy I always said goodbye in my heart." Sometimes Peter was overwhelmed with appreciation for his daughter.

"You know Amy, I believed I heard you. And I should have let you know somehow that I heard you in my heart. I hope you can always hear my heart telling you how much I love you."

Amy started to giggle and then she said, "Oh, Oh, Daddy. Now you're starting to get all mushy. I love you too from my heart. I've got to go. Debbie's ready to start school. Bye."

Peter sat there a moment. He knew he had tears in his eyes, but he didn't care. He was just a pushover when it came to his girls.

Lil was watching him, "Are you alright?"

Peter said, "Yes, I'm fine. Our daughter just told me I was getting all mushy. You both do that to me you know. How can I be this strong head of the house figure when I keep getting all emotional?"

Lil came over and put her arms around her husband and said, "I wouldn't change a thing. I kind of like my men to be sensitive and a bit sentimental."

Peter grabbed his coat and headed for the door, "I better get out of here before I start bawling. Be sure to call me when you find out what it is that Melody has brought you." He kissed Lil goodbye and then headed to work . . . .

At the Millers, the girls were settling down to their school work. Amy was pretty much caught up now and the two studied well together as long as they kept their focus. If they got tickled about something, then you were sure to lose them to a bundle of giggles.

Debbie knew that. So she kept things serious at least until break time. The girls were having some juice and crackers when Amy asked Debbie, "Aunt Debbie, do you think that we can make a choice like Miss Pat did, by pretending that God has his hand on our shoulder?"

Debbie had already considered that question, "Yes Amy, I do. In fact I think it's a great idea, because you're showing the Lord that you want and need His help."

Missy frowned and commented very seriously. "I agree that it's a really good idea and besides you won't make a mistake if you follow that rule." Then she crossed her arms and nodded her head, as if to put a punctuation mark on what she said.

Debbie thought she should add, "Yes, you won't make a mistake as long as you are sincere and you're acting from your heart. Because God cares for us and He likes for us to invite Him to be a part of our decisions." . . . .

Back at the Iversons, Lil kept looking at her watch. It was getting close to ten o'clock and Lil could hardly wait. She was very curious as to what it could be that Melody was bringing her.

At just a couple of minutes before ten the doorbell rang. Lil opened the door to find Melody standing there with nothing in her hands except her purse and it was a very small purse. Lil thought it must be a piece of jewelry, or perhaps a letter.

Lil invited Miss Harris into the front room where she had hot tea and sweet rolls waiting. After they exchanged the usual formalities, in which Melody had asked Lil to call her by her first name and Lil had said the same. Melody began with, "If it would be alright I would like to tell you just a bit about how I came to be so close to Miss Pat?"

Lil nodded and said, "Of course, in fact I've wondered about your story. I know you mentioned that Patricia took you in."

"Yes she did and I had absolutely no one else to turn to. In fact, at that time I wasn't really sure I even believed that God was real. I knew my mother had believed and I had thought, (I hope for my mother's sake that there really is a God.)

"Anyway about my story, I was pregnant by a boy that I was convinced I loved and I was sure he must love me too. He had made all these promises about how much he needed me and how I made him want to be a better person. I know now that everything he said was just a line he used to get what he wanted from me.

"When I told him I was pregnant, he suddenly had this bright idea of how he could go to California and make big money for me and the kid. But I knew he couldn't get away from me fast enough.

"Then my father kicked me out of the house. So I was very much alone, with no money and no help. It was at this timed that I met Miss Pat at a soup kitchen. She would stop in and bring them food and blankets to give to people. I'm sure she also gave them money. That seemed to be her whole purpose in life. She was always giving and trying to meet other people's needs.

"She took me home. At first I think even she thought it would only be temporary, but then something between us just clicked. And even after I lost my baby, Miss Pat wanted me to stay. I was so grateful. And it was Miss Pat who also introduced me to faith in God.

"I lived with her for almost six years, until I got my Degree in Nursing and then I got a job at a hospital that was too far away to commute every day. After I moved out I would still come over every weekend. We had become very close, but I always got the feeling that Miss Pat never quite felt free to just give in and embrace love again. I suppose it was because she had lost so much.

"The love was there though and she showed me in every other way. She just didn't use the words. She would send me cards to say what she felt. Time went on and at the age of thirty, I got married to Bill Harris. It was a good marriage and we were happy for nineteen years, but then Bill was killed in an auto accident. We never had any children.

"So I found myself back with Miss Pat. She needed a companion and nurse and I needed a friend to stave off the loneliness. So we just picked up right where we left off and I was her companion from then on. It was during this time, that she told me God had told her that someday she was to pass the book on. She always said she would know who the right person was. Miss Pat was very happy when David's letter came, partly because of her age; she was beginning to worry just a bit."

"But then Miss Pat just laughed and told me, 'I should have remembered (that *God is always right on time*).' Then she said, 'Meli, these are the right people; I want them to have my book.' And then a little later she told me, 'Meli, I want Lil Iverson to have my journals'."

Lil wasn't sure she heard right, "Journals? I know you mentioned that Patricia had written in a journal around the time that Thomas had made a decision to join the Navy, but I had no idea she was still keeping a journal."

Melody said, "Oh yes, in fact Patricia started keeping a journal after she went out on her own. The reason I didn't get them to you sooner was because I had to wait until her Estate was settled, just in case they should ask for them. However, about two weeks ago they signed a release so now I'm free to let you have them."

Lil asked, "Melody have you read these journals?"

"Yes, Miss Pat asked me to read them through the years. At first I was uncomfortable with the idea but then I came across places where she talked about (her dear companion). And I realized that she was using the journals to tell me how much she appreciated our friendship. She knew, by having me read the journals, I would be blessed.

"Lil there are three journals altogether. The first binder is from her personal life. You would think it would be very thick but after Thomas died she only wrote down truly special things.

"Sometimes she wrote only a few words, maybe a prayer or a poem; other times she would write nearly a page. This often happened on days she held as special for her and Thomas. Then there might be a poem or a few words on little William's birthday.

"She wrote occasionally about her father, usually on the anniversary of his death. She also wrote letters to her father and to Thomas, just as if they could still read them.

"In the other two binders she wrote maybe a dozen or so extended stories. These were about some of the girls that stayed at the home; girls that perhaps she grew more attached to. She never used real names because each girl would pick a name when she came to stay at the home. And from that time on they were always referred to by that name.

"They would pick simple names, like Mary, May, Betty, and Jean. By using these names, it gave them privacy and it also protected their reputations, as some of the girls came from very difficult situations. One thing she always recorded in these journals was when one of the girls made a commitment to the Lord. Miss Pat had a heart of gold when it came to these, young woman. They became her life and her ministry."

Lil had listened intently to what Melody said. After a while she asked, "Melody why me? Why did she think I should have these journals? I'm not a writer, if she had a book in mind and we never even met. So why did she pick me?"

Melody waited before she answered, "Lil, I'm pretty sure I know why she wanted you to have the journals, having read them myself. There are things in her personal journal that I am sure will bless you and your family. I will tell you that you share some similar experiences. I don't want to second guess what Miss Pat had in mind. Her instructions were simply, to give you the journals."

Lil finally asked, "Why didn't she just give them to you? That would seem more logical since you were her close friend."

"I had already read them and I've been very blessed by doing so. No Lil, she knew exactly what she was doing. Let me leave them with you and remember she said clearly, *'I want Lil Iverson to have my journals'*. Pray about it Lil, but I'm sure if you will just read Pat's personal journal, you will understand."

Lil had finally accepted the journals. Even though she wasn't sure she could allow herself to read them. Melody went out to her car and brought them in.

Before she left she had turned to Lil and said, "Miss Pat knew what she was doing. I am sure of that, especially after meeting you. You are very strong spiritually and so was my dear friend. I'm pretty sure you will read the journals. And when you do you'll get to know her better and you will agree with me, that you would have liked each other very much."

Melody embraced Lil and then she added, "Lil, you're going to be blessed as you read, I promise."

Lil was still trying to dissuade Melody, "But the only thing that Patricia knew about me came from Debbie's letter."

"Well then, there lies your answer." And with that she got in her car and drove off.

Lil stood in the door watching Melody drive away before she finally closed the door. Then she walked back into Peter's office were she had put the journals. She picked up the phone and called Peter.

Chapter Twenty Five

When Lil told Peter about the journals. He responded just the way she figured he would. "Did you say journals? Are you saying that Patricia kept journals?"

Lil laughed at her husband's reaction to the news. "That was exactly my reaction too. Peter, I went ahead and took them, but I'm not sure why. It was just that Melody was so insistent that I have them. She told me they would bless me, but how can I read someone else's personal journals. Peter, I just don't know what to do."

Peter said, "Why don't you just leave them for now and we'll take this to the Lord later . . . . And don't forget that we have something very special to tell Amy tonight. What do you say to all of us going out to celebrate after we've told her?"

Lil relaxed a little and then she said, "That sounds like a great idea. Thank you, Peter." . . . .

By the time Lil had eaten a light lunch, it was time for Debbie to bring Amy home. The girls came in both talking at the same time. Lil said, "Why don't you girls go out and get some sunshine and maybe burn off some on that energy."

The girls both put their fist in the air and said, "Yes!"

After the girls left, Lil and Deb settled down with some tea. Lil told Debbie about the journals.

"Deb, I don't know what to do. I'm still trying to understand, why me?"

"Lil, I have no problem understanding why Miss Pat wanted you to have them. You are very spiritual. Don't you know that? If it hadn't been for you, David and I might not have gotten saved."

"Deb, a lot of that goes to Peter. He's the one that witnessed to David all the time."

Debbie sat there amazed by her friend's humility. "Oh come on Lil, it was your witness in the hospital that started the whole thing off. You have to know that."

Lil thought over everything that had happened over the last few months. "Debbie, it just seems like such an intrusion into Patricia's privacy."

Debbie knew in her heart that Lil would make the right decision. Lil would take it to the Lord like she did everything else, and He would give her the answer.

After Debbie and Missy had gone home, Lil told Amy they were going out for spaghetti dinner. "That's great, but what's the occasion?" Lil wondered if Amy suspected what they were going to tell her.

Just then Peter came in through the back door and said, "How are my girls? Are you ready to go eat?"

Amy, in many ways still a five year old, jumped into her father's arms. "Yes Daddy. But what are we celebrating? Mommy didn't know."

Peter found that amusing, he responded with, "Oh I think your mother knows alright. You know don't you Lil?"

He was teasing both of them now. Amy said, "I knew it! I knew there was something. Tell me Mommy, please."

Lil had to laugh at her husband and her daughter the way they played off each other. "Okay you two. Are you ready for some really great news?"

Both Peter and Amy were nodding their heads vigorously. Peter piped up, "Yes Mommy, please tell us."

Lil just shook her head at her husband's teasing. She went to the drawer and got out the tissue wrapped booties and handed them to Amy.

Amy took them and slowly opened the tissue. Then suddenly Amy began to shed huge crocodile tears. "Oh Mommy, is it true? Are we getting a blessing from the fountain?"

Lil was a little surprised by Amy's reaction. It was unusual for her to be this emotional. Perhaps some of Missy was rubbing off on her daughter.

"Daddy I am so happy. I had almost given up, but God did it. He answered my prayers. Oh thank you God, thank you."

Lil looked at Peter and said, "Well maybe she hadn't guessed, I thought she might have."

Peter asked, "Amy, are you sure you didn't guess?"

Amy was reacting just about like her dad had. She was skipping around the living room. "No way Daddy, I had pretty much given up. But we should never give up, right?"

Lil was still quite surprised by Amy's reaction. She put her arm around her daughter and asked, "Amy honey, are you all right?"

Amy nodded her head and answered, "I'm fine Mommy, I'm just really, really happy." Amy was still blubbering (with happiness), as they headed out the door to go and celebrate.

Amy was up at the crack of dawn. Lil could hear her rummaging around in her bedroom. Lil got up quietly, so as not to wake Peter. She put on her slippers and went down the hall to Amy's room. She found Amy on her hands and knees pulling things out from under her bed.

"What is it honey? What are you looking for?" Amy looked up at her mother and started crying again. Lil sat down on the bed and pulled her daughter on to her lap, "What is it Amy? It's not like you to be so emotional. Please tell me what's going on."

Amy looked into Lil's eyes and said, "I was afraid that God thought I was being selfish because I wanted you to have a baby. And then I gave up and I shouldn't ever give up. Mommy, I was so happy when you told me about the baby. Am I a bad person? I just wanted to have a baby sister or brother so much, but I don't want to be bad."

Lil felt like crying right along with Amy now, "No darling, of course you're not bad. God isn't mad at you. Don't you know how much He loves you? How much we all love you? And you were not being selfish. Both your daddy and I want this baby very much."

Amy began to quiet down, "Okay Mommy."

Lil wiped the tears away from Amy's face with a tissue. Then she asked, "What were you looking for honey? Maybe I know where it is."

Amy was getting herself composed, "I was looking for that fluffy white teddy bear I used to have because I want to save it for the baby."

Lil got up from the bed and went into Amy's closet; she reached up on the top shelf and pulled down the fluffy white teddy bear and handed it to Amy.

Amy took the teddy and gave her mom a big hug and a kiss. "Oh thank you, Mommy."

Peter had heard the voices and he stuck his head in the door and asked, "What's going on in here?"

Amy who finally had herself under control said, "Its complicated Daddy. Maybe Mommy can tell you later."

Lil had to laugh. She turned Amy toward the bathroom, "Go get ready for breakfast, we're having pancakes."

With that, Amy was gone and Peter stood there scratching his head. "What just happened here?"

Lil gave Peter a kiss on the cheek as she brushed past him, "Don't worry dear. I'll fill you in later. Right now, I need to go get the pancakes started." . . . .

After breakfast, Lil went into Peter's office and stood there staring at the journals. "Oh Lord tell me what to do."

Peter stepped up behind Lil and put his hand of her shoulder. (It was like a bolt of lightning.) Lil turned to Peter, "I think you just gave me the answer on how to approach this journal thing."

Peter said, "But Lil, I didn't do anything."

Lil turned and gave Peter a knowing smile and said, "Yes you did. You put your hand on my shoulder."

It only took Peter a couple of seconds to get it, "Ah . . . . the hand on the shoulder thing. Do you think it will work for us?"

"We'll soon find out. Are you ready to pray with me about this? I can believe that God has his hand on my shoulder."

Peter agreed and they stood next to each other as Peter asked God for wisdom, "Oh Lord, please give us wisdom on how we should handle Patricia's journals. Help Lil to hear you clearly so she can make the very best choice. Thank you for being here with us. Your word says, in *Matt. 18: 20, (For where two or three, are gathered together in my name, there I am in the midst of them.)* Thank you for making the way clear. We ask this in Jesus name. Amen."

Lil looked up from the prayer, "Thank you Peter and now we just wait for the answer."

It was a couple of days later. And since it was Saturday and Peter didn't have to be on the phones at the office, he and Amy had gone to watch David coach a little league game and of course Missy would be there too. Then after the game they were all going to get hamburgers. Peter had set this up to give Lil some time to work on her fall line without distractions.

Lil was in her little office working on some sketches. She had to start work on the fall line even though it was only the second of April. She needed to have the designs ready for the seamstress, so they had plenty of time to work out the kinks.

She was working on something she knew would look great on Debbie after she had the baby. She was thinking about how excited Deb had been the night she had taken her to see "Lil's Fashions". Lil had grown very fond of Debbie.

Lil frowned and thought, now where is that other sketch pad. With the sketch that shows the back of the dress? She had been using a blue sketch pad. She liked to change the color of the pad she used with each new season. It helped to keep them separated. I know I had it yesterday. Oh wait, now I remember, Peter called and asked me to look up a contract in his office. I bet I carried it in there and left it.

Lil hurried to Peter's office and looked around his files. I know this is where I was looking yesterday. The paper he needed was right here in these black folders. Lil opened each one looking for her sketch but it just wasn't there. She sat down in Peter's chair and she looked on the desk. There was no blue sketch pad.

Lil finally gave up. She stood up and reached back to straighten the black folders and that's when she saw the edge of the blue paper sticking out from one of Patricia's journals. She pulled the journal out from the pile and the blue pad was stuck right in the front of the journal. Lil put the journal on Peter's desk and she could see about two inches of the blue pad sticking out.

She thought, (Could Peter have stuck it there?) But then she completely dismissed the idea. Peter would never do that. She didn't understand it but she would just open the journal and retrieve her sketch pad. Lil carefully opened the journal and lifted the sketch pad out of the way. She just couldn't help it; her eyes fell on the open page. She could hardly believe what she saw, the journal was opened to Feb. 14, 1942 and there it was in plain sight, the entry written by Patricia.

"My dearest Tom, My heart aches. Knowing that in a few days you must leave me here, to go and do what you must for your Country. Tom darling, I will never say goodbye, I will only say, later. I will see you later. Until then my heart will simply wait. Darling, I will keep you in my heart and in my prayers always." Patricia

Lil found it a little hard to breathe. She sure didn't know what to think. The one thing she knew for sure was that this was not a coincidence. She thought, (Okay if God can send heavenly lilacs to the earth He could certainly use her sketch pad to direct her to the journals.)

Lil looked at her watch; she had several hours before they would all come back. They had planned to watch a movie together and have some sandwiches. She sat motionless, just staring at Pat's entry in the journal not sure what to do next.

Finally she spoke, "Okay Lord you have my attention. Now what do you want me to do?"

As Lil thought about all the love ones Pat had lost especially when she was so young, she felt her heart break for poor Patricia. "All of that loss and she was so alone. I've always had Peter, but who did Patricia have?"

Then Lil heard these words in her spirit, "She always had Me, I never left her."

Lil straighten up, "Yes, of course she had you, because you promised us in your word, Hebrews 13:5 (*I will never desert you, nor will I ever forsake you). Lord forgive me, I do know you were always there with Miss Pat."

Lil had heard the Lord's voice before. When the doctors had given up on Amy, the Lord had spoken plainly, "Don't ever give up on Amy!" Lil had drawn strength from those words and she and Peter had held on to them until they had Amy back.

Lil looked at the journal again, wondering what to do. And then she remembered something Melody had said, right before she drove off. Lil had commented to Melody that, all Pat knew about her had come from Debra's letter. And Melody had said, "Well then, there is your answer."

Lil couldn't believe she had missed it. She grabbed Peter's desk phone and called Debbie. Debbie answered, "Hi, this is Debbie."

Lil had to take a deep breath, "Deb this is Lil. I need you to do something for me, right away."

Deb said, "Okay sure, what do you need?"

"Deb, I don't have time to explain, but I need for you to look up what you said in the letter to Patricia. I need to know exactly what you said about me."

Deb spoke right up, "Sure hold on a minute," Deb pulled a copy of the letter from the desk, "Okay I've got it. I said, *(Lil Iverson is Amy's mother, and she was a visitor to the heavenly Garden of Blessings. She asked me to tell you of the incredible peace she always felt while she was there. Then I told her about the lilacs from the heavenly garden.)* That's it Lil. What's this all about anyhow?"

Lil said, "That's all you said? That's certainly not very much. Debbie I've got to go. I will explain it when you come over later."

With that Lil was gone and Debbie was left holding the phone. She said, "That was odd, I wonder what's going on."

Lil hung up the phone, "I don't get it? All Patricia knew about me was that I had been a visitor to the heavenly garden; Melody said that we shared a similar experience. What does that mean, Lord? What did we share? (*Then it came to Lil, what they might have in common.*) . . . .

Lil picked up the journal still opened to Feb. 14, 1942. She flipped the pages. There was a prayer, and then a few lines about a sunset, that Pat wished she could share with Tom.

"Tom there is the most beautiful sunset tonight. Oh how I wish you were here to share it with me. I can't begin to tell you how much I miss you. But then you must already know that. I begin and end each day with a prayer for you." All my love, Patricia

On the next page there was a copy of a poem from Tom.

THE LEGEND OF THE FORGET-ME-NOT

When to the flowers so beautiful

The Father gave a name,

There came a little blue-eyed one~

All timidly it came~

And standing at the Father's feet,

And gazing in His face,

It said with low and timid voice,

And yet with gentle grace,

"Dear Lord, the name thou gavest me,

Alas, I have forgot."

The Father kindly looked on him

And said, "Forget-me-not." Anon

"Oh Tom, what a dear poem, I will keep it always. Thank you, for putting it in my Bible. What a sweet surprise for me to find. And you can rest assured that I will (forget—you-not), simply because you are forever planted in my heart. Right where I showed you I would keep you. I'm forever yours, Patricia

Lil kept looking, but mostly it was just Patricia talking and sharing with the people she loved. She was using the journal to keep her loved ones, close to her. Lil read a line written to Tom.

"Oh Tom, I pray that you are aware of just how very much I love and need you."

Lil skimmed over the pages. She found the place where Pat had gotten Tom's letter. It was heart wrenching to read where Patricia pleaded for forgiveness.

"Oh Tom, I am so ashamed. I lost all heart when I lost you. I turned my back on God. That's something I never thought I would do. Tom I pray that you forgive me; I was just so lost and depressed . . . . Then, thankfully, I received your last letter, dated May 1, 1942. It made me so happy to know that you knew about the baby. Tom, I believe that your letter saved my life and the life of our baby. I snapped out of the depression and did what you asked me to do. I've taken good care of us Tom. I've even been drinking lots and lots of milk. I've done the very best I could, but oh how we've miss you." With all my love, Pat

It was hard for Lil to read these very private missives, but she told herself it was what Patricia had wanted. Then she found the place where little William's birth was recorded. November 15, 1942

"Dearest Tom, I must tell you about our little William. I think he must be the most precious baby ever born. He's perfect in every way, because he already looks like his Daddy. He's very tiny right now and yet he is so perfect, but then I already told you that. Oh Thomas I so hope you can see him." Love Always, Pat

Pat continued the next day . . . .

"Tom, I just can't stop looking at our dear son, he is such a joy. You should see his dear little mouth. A nurse told me that you might be able to look down from heaven and see him. If you can, I know how very proud you must be. We both send our love."

Then on the third day, there were tears on the page, as Pat had written . . . .

"Dearest Tom, my heart is breaking yet again, for I have lost our dear Willy after only three days. Tom I need to believe that he is there with you. Watch over him for me and please darling, tell him how much I love him. And be sure and tell him I will see you both later." I am eternally yours, Patricia.

There was very little written for the next year, mostly a few poems and some prayers. Then, Lil turned to Nov. 15, 1943 . . . .

Chapter Twenty Six

After the game Peter, David and the girls were finishing up their lunch, when David's cell phone rang. Seeing it was Deb, he answered, "Hello, love of my life. What's going on?"

Debbie laughed, and said, "I like the sound of that. Hey, I got a kind of strange call from Lil earlier and I was wondering if Peter might know what it's all about."

David said, "Define what you mean when you say strange . . . ."

Debbie laughed again, and said, "Why don't you just let me talk to Peter for a minute and then I won't have to explain it twice."

David handed the phone to Peter, "Its Deb. She wants to ask you something."

"Hi Debbie, what can I do for you?" Peter listened to Deb and then he began to nod, "I bet this has something to do with Pat's journal. Was she upset?"

Debbie said, "No I wouldn't say upset, she was just really focused. Are you guys about finished there? And when can I expect David to pick me up? I'm kind of anxious to find out what's going on. It's been several hours since she called."

Peter told Deb they were finishing up and David would be there soon to pick her up, while Peter headed on home with the girls.

David asked, "What was that all about? Is everything alright?"

Peter said, "I'm sure everything is fine. And I'm reasonably sure that it has something to do with Patricia's journal." Then he thought to himself, I would really like to know what's going on. I can't help but worry just a little. I sure hope you're okay Lil. Peter sent a silent prayer to the Lord.

As Peter was driving home, he couldn't stop thinking about what Debbie had said about Lil's call. He wasn't worried, but he knew how emotional this thing with Patricia had been for her.

Peter was a little concerned that Lil might have decided to read the journal and that reading it might have upset her. Peter also knew that Lil was a strong woman. She wasn't easily upset. And anyway, they had prayed about this and asked God for wisdom. "I know you are right there with her, Lord."

Peter drove into the drive way. The girls were out of the car and heading for the house when Peter stopped them and said, "Would you girls mind playing on the swings for a little while?" They both turned and went running for the swing set.

Peter went in through the back of the house and called Lil's name, but he heard nothing. He went to her office and found it empty. "Lil where are you sweetheart?"

Peter headed for his office where he knew the journals were kept. He opened the door and there sat Lil with tears streaming down her cheeks. She was holding a journal in her arms. Peter looked at her face and she had the same glow that she always had, when she had just come back from the garden. He entered the room and asked, "Lil honey are you okay?" He knelt down beside her.

"Oh Peter, I understand now. I know why she wanted me to have her journals . . . . I couldn't find my blue sketch pad this morning and I remembered that you had called me yesterday and asked me to look something up in your files. I figured I might have left the pad in here, so I came to look for it and Peter it was sticking out from this journal. I knew that neither one of us had put it there, so I pulled out the journal to look. And Peter, the blue pad was marking the place where Pat had written the goodbye note to Thomas. Remember she had written it while Thomas was gone for his training?"

Peter had sat down in the other chair, "Yes I remember. Melody had included it in her letter telling us about Pat. Is that when you called Debbie?" Lil looked a little surprised. Peter explained, "Debbie called just a while ago, I think she was a little worried."

Lil nodded, "Yes, I called Debbie because I was still trying to figure out why me. I remembered that Melody had told me something the day she was here. She said that Pat and I shared a similar experience and that the answer lay in what Patricia knew about me.

"I had thought the only thing she knew about me was what Debbie had written. But then, I finally realized that she couldn't have made the decision to give me the journals from Debbie's letter, because Patricia went to be with the Lord right after she got the things we sent her. She never had another chance to talk with Melody. So it had to have been David's letter.

Peter looked confused. Lil explained further. "It was the timing Peter, David's letter was written several weeks earlier. David had told Pat that I had been a visitor to the heavenly garden and that I had also read the book "*The Garden of Blessings*" there. That had to be when she made the decision to give all of us the book and to give me her journals.

"The *key*, to her giving me the journals was that I had been a visitor to the heavenly garden. Once I knew what to look for. I started looking and I found it easily. Peter it's incredible. I'd like for everyone to hear this. Are they here?"

Peter told her, "David and Debbie are most likely on the way and the girls are playing outside."

Lil said, "Okay, why don't you go and sort of prepare everyone. You can tell them how the Lord led me to look in the journal and how He marked the special place. Then when they are all here, I'll bring the journal out and share what I found. Oh Peter, Melody was right; this is going to bless everyone." . . . .

Peter agreed it was a good idea, so he went to gather the troops and to get them ready to hear another amazing story.

Peter filled everyone in on how God had led Lil to the journal and how she had discovered something remarkable there. And that Lil wanted to share what she had found with rest of them.

Amy said, "Wow, I think that is so neat how God led Mommy to look at Miss Pat's journal."

Missy piped up and said, "I'll bet Auntie Lil asked God to help and she pretended he had his hand on her shoulder. And that's why he helped her to find the right place in the journal."

Debbie, who could hardly wait to find out what Lil had discovered said, "This is all so supernatural. The Lord just keeps on surprising us."

Finally Lil came out with the journal. She smiled and said, "Hi, I know we've all been wondering what was in Patricia's journals. And you also know I've been trying to figure out why she wanted me to have them. Especially, since I didn't even know her.

"Peter and I have been seeking the Lord's help ever since Melody brought the journals to us. And today, things finally began to fall into place. This is really remarkable and it also answers a lot of the question we've all had. Particularly these pages I am going to read, I'm very certain they will have a special meaning to every person here. I'll try to read it exactly the way Patricia wrote it."

They all sat with their eyes on Lil, as she began to read from Patricia's journal. Lil smiled and then added, "Remember these are Patricia's words." Lil skips the date and begins to read . . . .

Nov. 15 1943

The book I'm reading is a <u>Children's Book of Poems,</u> and I am sitting in a lovely garden with the most beautiful flowers all around me. I begin to read . . . .

The Playful Sunbeam

There is a little sunbeam, who likes to play with me,

And when he comes he finds me waiting patiently.

I really like to watch him as he skips from tree to tree.

I know he must be truly happy, to be so very free.

But he moves about so quickly, I simply can't keep up,

And I'm sure this is on purpose, because he likes to tease,

But he says, "No tis not I who moves so quickly,

It has to be the breeze! Jme

I hear someone calling me. I look up from my reading . . . .

"Patricia . . . . Patricia, I was so hoping you would get to come. The angels said you might be able. Come with me darling. There's something I want to show you, something very special."

I was so stunned that I just sat there for a minute not sure what I was seeing, but it seemed so real . . . . I was actually seeing my beloved Tom . . . .

I jumped up from the bench and hurried to follow. "Tom, is it truly you or am I dreaming?"

Tom put his finger to his lips indicating that I shouldn't ask question. "Does it really matter Patricia? I think we should just enjoy *this*, whether it is a dream or reality, to us right now it is a blessing. Is it not?"

I started laughing. As I hurried to keep up, "Yes of course you are right; we should simply enjoy *this*." Thomas took us down a path and through some lilac bushes.

It was then that I heard the sounds like babies when they try to talk; we stepped out into a clearing . . . . What I saw took my breath away. There on a big blue blanket was the most beautiful baby I have ever seen and he was sitting up very straight and moving his arms about like he was playing a drum.

Sitting with him were several young girls who seemed intent on getting him to giggle. And he was being very obliging, as the baby sounds he made soon turned to giggles and then to squeals of delight.

"Oh Tom, its Willy isn't it? It's our beloved Willy." Tom was beside me now. We didn't touch but we were able to communicate. I felt the most incredible love coming from him to me.

He nodded and said, "Yes Patricia. That is our precious William. I am watching over him, just as you asked me to. And as you can see he is well cared for."

Just then Willy spotted us and he began bouncing up and down. And then something truly remarkable happened. He began to say what sounded like, "Ma mah, ma mah," and then more squeals.

I looked at Tom who was grinning at me. "Tom did he just say *what it* sounded like? Well no matter. I choose to believe that he called me, 'Mama'. Oh Tom, this is so wonderful."

"I'm so glad that you got to be here Patricia. Always remember that we are here waiting. And Pat, there is no sorrow here, only the joy of the Lord. I love you Pat. We both love you and we will see you later darling . . . ."

Suddenly I wake up. I am sitting in a screened in porch. My roommates and I have made a big bouquet of flowers from crepe paper, to which we have added some perfume . . . . *It's not a garden at all. I'm not in a garden.*

I sit there trying to figure out what has just happened. And I finally realize I have just been a visitor to a *heavenly garden* in a dream about my dear William, on his very first birthday. It was all so vivid. I remember Tom was there with our little Willy.

I knew I needed to write this down while it was still fresh. So I have hurriedly recorded it in my journal.

"Oh thank you Lord, for this glorious gift. I don't know if this will ever happen again, but I am overjoyed and so grateful that it happened today." When I finished recording what I had just experienced, I got down on my knees to properly thank the Lord.

"Dear Lord Jesus, for me to simply say thank you seems completely inadequate. Lord, you've taken a day that would have torn at my heart and instead you have given me a beautiful blessing. Just like in the Bible, you have given to me. *(Beauty for ashes, the oil of joy for mourning, the garment of praise for the spirit of heaviness.) Isaiah 61:3 KJV* Lord, thank you for showing me that my love ones are there safe with you. And that one day we will all be reunited, in your Heavenly Garden."

When Lil finished no one spoke for a few minutes and then Peter said, "You were right Lillian that did truly bless me. I believe that might even get the attention of a non-believer."

Lil jerked her head up, "Lillian, since when do you call me Lillian? I don't remember you ever using anything other than Lil?" They all had a good laugh about that.

Peter defended himself, by saying, "I guess I just got so caught up in the time period, I was actually picturing them, as they might have looked back in their day, and then Lillian just seemed to fit," he paused for effect and added, "Lillian my love."

David just shook his head and then spoke up next, "Peter, sometimes you're really too much. Lil, I definitely got blessed. And to just think, I started the search for the book on a lark. Wow! Do you think it's possible that I might have been following a leading from the Holy Spirit?"

Debbie was next to jump in, "I bet it was the Lord stirring you up and then he just kept pulling you along. I am so glad that you contacted Miss Pat. What an incredible blessing for all of us."

The girls had been very quiet, but they were both wiping tears away. Amy said, "Remember in our letter, I told Miss Pat that there were many gardens in heaven, but I guess she already knew that."

Then last but not least, little Missy was heard from, "Auntie Lil, I'm so happy that Miss Pat got to see where little Willy was. So she would know he was alright and that someday they'd all be together."

Then Debbie asked, "Is there more? Did she get to visit again?"

Lil said, "There is more, but I stopped once I found this. I think we'll save the rest for another day and remember there are also the other two journals where Pat wrote about some of the young women she helped. I'm sure there's plenty there to keep us all guessing for quite a while."

Peter piped up, "It seems Miss Pat was full of surprises. And speaking of surprises . . . . Lil and I have one to share." Peter glanced at Lil and saw just a slight bit of coloring in her cheeks. Or maybe that was just a glow.

Both David and Debbie had stopped talking and were looking at Lil expectantly.

Amy started to giggle, but then she tried real hard to suppress it.

Lil was definitely blushing now. "Okay everyone, I may as well give the announcement. Peter and I are going to have a baby and he or she is due on November 15th."

Little Missy let out a gasp and then covered her mouth. When everyone turned to look at her, she whispered almost reverently, "That's little Willy's birthday."

Lil nodded; she had realized that, the minute the doctor had given her that date. She simply said, "Yes, that is a very special day and if our baby comes on that day, it will be even more special."

Amy went over and hugged Missy. They both were chatting away with excitement about the fact that they were both going to be big sisters.

Debbie started weeping with joy for her friend. David was slapping Peter on the back. All in all, things looked very good for the Iversons and the Millers . . . .

Lil thought of Pat's journals and couldn't help wondering what other surprises they might hold. She sent a little prayer to the Lord, "Thank you, for allowing me to spend time with Amy in one of your beautiful gardens." Then she joined her family and friends to celebrate the good news.

Epilogue

———————————◆———————————

It was Christmas Eve and the Miller's new house was completely decked out for the season. David and Debbie had decided they needed more room after Matthew Peter Miller was born, so they had bought a bigger house very close to Peter and Lil's.

There was a big Christmas tree and a lot of holly. There were Christmas wreaths on the front and back doors. Festive bows and mistletoe hung from the door ways. And of course there were lots of packages under the tree. There were quite a few presents for baby Matt, who promised to be a real charmer with his golden blond coloring, just like Debbie's . . . .

Everyone would be there soon, including the newest addition to the Iverson family, Patricia Anna Iverson, who was indeed born on November 15TH, making that day very special indeed . . . .

Missy had spent the night with Amy and the girls were all excited because they had both asked for ice skates. The skates were to be used on the Iverson's pond. And it had been just cold enough that the pond was frozen just right for ice skating . . . .

Right now Missy was sitting in front of little Patty Ann and she kept saying over and over, "Oh Amy she is so pretty." And there was no doubt she was beautiful, her hair was a deeper red than Lil's and Amy's, showing a little more likeness to Peter, with his sandy brown hair.

Amy was also taken with her little sister. But Amy had laughed at her mother, when Lil had sat her down and said, "Honey, you do understand don't you, that babies don't really come from fountains?"

Amy had shook her bronze curls and said, "Mommy, of course I know that. I am eight years old now, you know. Anyway it's their spirits that come from God."

Lil was always just a little taken back by Amy's and Missy's insight into spiritual matters. Perhaps it was a maturity that came from their having been in the garden.

And so it happened on this Christmas Eve that both the Iversons and the Millers each embraced the double blessings, of having their daughters back and having babies Matt and Patty to celebrate.

And naturally there was much thanksgiving going up to heaven, for the birth of their Dear Savior, Jesus Christ . . . . And if you listened really carefully you just might hear angels singing. *"Glory to God in the highest, and on earth peace, good will toward men."* Luke 2:14 KJV

There were also those journals of Patricia's. Who knows, perhaps someday Lil just might write a book. After all, they did have a lot to share. She could talk about the heavenly garden, both from her perspective and from Patricia's. The girls would certainly have something to add. Who knew what the New Year would bring.

As for right now, Lil felt that her cup was running over and her heart was full. Lil gave one more look at Patricia's journals, before turning off the lights in Peter office and heading to the front room to get everyone ready to head over to the Millers.

"Lord, this is truly a very special Christmas Eve. Thank you once again for allowing me to be (A Visitor to Heaven's Garden of Blessings)."

The End

The Poem: <u>The Legend Of The Forget-Me-Not</u>

The Author is Unknown

Was taken from the book of poems;

HEART THROBS Volume Two

IN PROSE AND VERSE

Published by

CHAPPLE PUBLISHING COMPANY, Ltd.

Boston, Mass., U.S.A.

Expressly for

WORLD SYNDICATE COMPANY

110 West Fortieth Street

New York City

Copyright, 1941